TERRA ELAN McVOY

Drive

Me

CRAZY

K:T: KATHERINE TEGEN BOOKS
An Imprint of HarperCollins Publishers

Katherine Tegen Books is an imprint of HarperCollins Publishers.

Drive Me Crazy
Copyright © 2015 by HarperCollins Publishers
All rights reserved. Printed in the United States of America.

Library of Congress Cataloging-in-Publication Data
McVoy, Terra Elan.
    Drive me crazy / Terra Elan McVoy. — First edition.
        pages   cm
    Summary: "When Lana's and Cassie's grandparents marry each other, the
girls find themselves stuck together on a crazy summer road trip that will change
the course of their friendship and their lives"— Provided by publisher.
    ISBN 978-0-06-232244-9
    [1. Grandparents—Fiction.   2. Cousins—Fiction.   3. Friendship—
Fiction.   4. Automobile travel—Fiction.   5. California—Fiction.]   I. Title.
PZ7.M478843Dr   2015   2014029061
[Fic]—dc23   CIP
                                                                         AC

Typography by Michelle Gengaro-Kokmen
16 17 18 19 20 CG/OPM   10 9 8 7 6 5 4 3 2 1
❖
First paperback edition, 2016

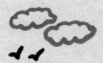

For everyone who's trying
to be a good friend to someone else

Chapter One

Lana

Wonderful is the only word I can use to describe it. We haven't even been in the car for an hour yet, and already we're singing at the top of our lungs, enjoying the sunshine streaming down through the sunroof, and letting the warm wind whip around us through the open windows. Me and Grandpa Howe have our arms dangling out (Grandma Tess has both hands on the wheel), and when I catch his eye in the passenger-side mirror, it's hard to tell whose smile is bigger. Being on the road bright and early for an eight-day trip together around California is fun and exciting enough, but that we're on the way to Monterey first, so my new stepcousin Cassie can join us, makes the whole day shimmer with excitement.

Admittedly it's hard not to have fun around my grandpa Howe and grandma Tess. The first thing I thought about Tess when she and Grandpa Howe started seeing each other was that she looked exactly like a girl on a merry-go-round in old picture books, except for all her wrinkles. Her vibrancy was a little overwhelming, actually—so different from my gentle nana Lilia, who had died two years before—but it didn't take long for me to really adore her. The first time she came with Grandpa Howe over to our house, Tess brought my mom a necklace she'd made of beach glass—the kind Mom would never buy for herself but always admires in shops. Immediately, Tess launched into a funny story about how she'd collected the glass on a private beach and almost got arrested for trespassing. By the time dinner and games were over, Mom and Dad and I already wanted her to be a part of our family.

Grandma Tess tells the best stories—some even better than Grandpa Howe, which I didn't think was possible. There are lots about her early California days as a hippie, but my favorites are about Cassie. I can't get enough of them. I'd heard so much about Cassie that by the time we finally met at our grandparents' wedding, I felt like we were already old friends. Well, sort of. But not nearly as close as we'll be by the end of this trip, I'm sure.

I'm about to ask, mid-song, how much farther it is to

Cassie's house when Grandma Tess waves her turquoise-laden hand at a sign that's zooming toward us.

"Ooh, here it is, Howie."

I'm not sure what she means, but Grandpa Howe apparently does. He reaches for his glasses and the map.

"Redwood City! They renovated the whole downtown," Grandma Tess explains to me. "It's so fun to imagine what a town was, and where it's come from, when you're looking at what it's hoping to be, don't you think?"

I nod and keep singing, mostly to hide the twinge of disappointment I feel. So far I love being swept up in Grandma Tess's adventures—it's part of why I'm excited about this trip—but not when it means taking the long way, with extra pauses, to get to Cassie. It's already been a whole month since the wedding, and I don't want to wait a second longer for our reunion. There are tons of things I want to discuss—the boyfriend she told me about at the reception, and all the things she's done this summer, not to mention what we'll do together over the next week—but I'm also keen to hit the reset button with her as soon as possible.

It's not that things were bad at Grandma Tess and Grandpa Howe's wedding. I know we hit it off (how could we not, accidentally showing up in the same dress?!), but toward the end, when the last dances were happening and everyone was helping to clean up, I thought she seemed embarrassed to be around me. Or mad, or something. Probably I was just being too chatty, which Mom and Dad both say I can get. (They've been saying it a lot more lately, since Mom's headaches started happening.) But I don't always have to be the one talking; I can be a good listener too. Or we can even hang out, not talking, the way Mom likes doing with her friend Beth. As soon as we finally see each other again, I know things will straighten out and Cassie and I will jump right back on track. We just need to *get* there.

As Grandpa Howe navigates Grandma Tess through the various stoplights and street signs of Redwood City, and we finally find a place to park, I try to remind myself that this *is* their honeymoon. It was beyond wonderful for them to want me and Cassie to be a part of it, so I need to go where I'm taken and be cheerful about it.

We get out of the car to stroll the sidewalks of downtown, and I try to look around with "interested eyes," as Dad likes to say. It's what he does when he meets a new landscaping client, instead of going in with particular expectations of his own. It works for him, I guess, because he and Mom have so many clients, but since there already is something I'm interested in—my new friend-slash-cousin Cassie—it's hard to be interested here, too.

Not for my grandparents, though.

"Look at that theater," Grandma Tess says, tugging Grandpa Howe down the sidewalk. "Gorgeous! I wonder what they have showing. What do you think, Lana? A luxurious morning matinee? With popcorn and Milk Duds, of course."

I glance at my watch. "Do they really show movies this early?" I ask, thinking of Cassie waiting for us to appear in her driveway in another hour.

Grandma Tess waves away my question, her billowy pink sleeve trailing after her tan, freckled arm. "Oh, I don't really want to spend that much time here, don't worry. I'm eager to get to Cassie, too. It was just a fleeting thought."

She beams at Grandpa Howe, and he puts his arm around her back. His other arm stretches out, gesturing for me to speed up and join them on his other side, so I do, and we walk together like that down the bricked sidewalk, gazing at the renovated theater and the shops along the street.

Maybe Dad's "interested eyes" trick kicks in, because a sign up ahead of us catches my eye: BRICK MONKEY.

"What about in here?" I say, pausing when we get to the wide front window.

Grandma Tess glances at the sign, and the art inside, and shrugs happily. Grandpa Howe holds the door open for us, and we cross into the dark, cool interior.

Most of the things in the store are big: big paintings, big modern-looking couches, big mirrors, big toothy smile on the lady who says hello to us. Near the back, however, there's a round table painted all over with flowers and covered with jewelry and accessories. On one side is a rack full of gauzy, hand-dyed scarves. I slide a pretty green one through my fingers, admiring the way the light catches the glossy metallic threads woven in. Cassie would like these, I think. Or at least, I can see her wearing one. I briefly consider buying it—a kind of Happy Vacation peace offering/ present—but when I turn the price tag over and consider my spending money for the whole trip, I decide maybe she would think it was too big a gesture, anyway. Too babyish and eager.

Still, I like everything on the table. I run my fingers gently across the necklace stands, and the little curved bowls holding earrings, round sparkling pins, delicate silver baubles and charms. A nearby trinket catches my eye: a rhinestone-covered bird, perched on a ribbon of silver that says, in stamped letters, *Be Your Own Peace*. I pick it up and hold the tiny, shining thing in my hand. Mom would like this. Or maybe, I would just like to get it for her. Something small and pretty she could hold in one of the giant pockets of her backpack or cargo pants, a glittering reminder to slow down, be peaceful.

It's a reminder she could really use. She and Dad are always busy with their landscaping business—they say it's seasonal but it's really not, because whenever they're not planting or planning, they're dealing with all the paper-work and finance stuff they can't get done while they're outdoors making people's properties prettier and more ecologically responsible. They're *always* busy, even at the dinner table.

Most of the time it's fun to listen to them, because Mom does amazing voices mimicking their clients, and Dad lights up as she talks, chortling and adding in his own bits. The last couple of weeks it hasn't been the same, though. Instead of funny stories of high-strung housewives, or fretting over whether or not they can get certain bushes locally, more and more it's Mom lying down with one of her headaches, or Dad and me being quiet so she's able to nap. Every day, there are moons of purple under her eyes that mean something's wrong. She says she's not any more tired than she usually is and that she's only asking more of me because I'm growing up so much, but she's never needed me to push the grocery cart in the store before. She steers, and I check the list. That's the way we've done it since I learned how to read. But the other day I was the one behind the cart, pulling things into the basket. She kept rubbing the side of her forehead, and I knew then there was another reason they were sending me with Grandpa Howe and Grandma Tess on this trip. Something scary. Something they don't want me to see.

"Why, that's pretty," Grandpa Howe says, putting his hand on my shoulder, startling me. "I like what it says."

I swallow, realizing that thinking about Mom in the grocery store has made a crying feeling happen in the back of my nose and eyes.

"Yeah." I nod. "I thought Mom might like it."

"Your mom might like what?" Grandma Tess says, coming over. "Oh, these scarves are beautiful." She slides one through her fingers like I did just a minute ago.

I take a breath. "She would like a lot of things in here," I say, trying to make my eyes happy.

Grandma Tess puts her hand on top of Grandpa Howe's, which is still resting on my shoulder. I can feel them looking at each other over my head. Can feel the happiness pouring off them, now mixed with a sudden concern about me. It's a feeling I don't like much—when people see that you're sad and then get sad for you, too.

I put the sparkling little bird back down in its bowl with the others.

"It's still early for me to be buying a bunch of souvenirs, right?" I say brightly. "We haven't even been two hours into this trip! Who knows what we'll find."

"That's right, of course," Grandma Tess says. "Who knows?" And then, in a gentle way that makes me want her to stop talking: "If you think it'd please your mother, I say go for it. Even if it just pleases you."

"I know what would please her." Grandpa Howe winks at me. "We find our way to the nearest ice cream cone, and then get ourselves back on the road."

I smile up at him, grateful that if he can tell the stuff about Mom is bothering me, he won't make a deal about it. I squeeze his hand lightly as we thank the lady behind the counter and head back into the sunshine, meandering around the main square until we find a frozen yogurt spot. It isn't as great as the house-made flavors we're used to at the Custard Cup down the street from Grandpa Howe and Grandma Tess's place—so close we can ride our bikes— but it is fun piling on as many crazy toppings as we can and then coming up with names for our hodgepodge sundaes.

We eat on the way to the car, finishing up right there in the parking lot instead of sitting and savoring, so we won't keep Cassie waiting any longer. Back in the car, I'm feeling a little better, though Mom is still on my mind. Grandpa Howe and Grandma Tess turn the music up and go back to their singing, but I stay quiet in the backseat, watching out the window. I'm used to Mom and Dad leaving me out of things sometimes—jokes or comments they think I won't understand or am not interested in—but as we drive farther from my home, I realize this is the first time they've ever sent me *away*. The more I think about it, the more I'm sure they're keeping something terrible from me.

I'm so distracted with all the awful things that could be wrong with Mom, and then trying to convince myself that I'm just overreacting like I do and surely it's none of those, that before I know it we're exiting off the highway again and driving through what must be Cassie's suburb. As I gaze out at all the expensive boutiques and classy restaurants, the big breezy houses and the sculpted lawns, some of my excitement about Cassie comes back, but I also feel a little intimidated. I knew Cassie was cool, but this is all much more sophisticated than our funky little neighborhood in Berkeley. If this is the way Cassie and all her friends live, then she's even more glamorous than I thought.

As we pull into her driveway—her house is bigger and fancier than some of my parents' wealthiest clients'—I take out my phone and quickly text Mom and Dad to say we've arrived in Monterey and that it's already a great trip. As soon as it's sent, I turn down the volume and tuck my phone back into my bag. Texting your parents every ten minutes, or rushing to the phone when they respond, is probably not Cassie's idea of sophisticated. Even though I feel a little twinge about it, I don't want to look dumb, and I certainly don't want Cassie to sense that anything's wrong. Then she'd be the one asking questions, and of course I could never lie to her. I don't want her pitying me. I want her to like me because of me, not whatever is going on at home.

Besides, I think, shutting the car door and following Grandma Tess and Grandpa Howe up to the front door, she'll be able to pity me plenty when Mom is dead.

Cassie

nfair would be one word for it. *Mortifying. Disgusting. Cruel and Unusual Punishment.* The list could go on, believe me.

Not only do I have to spend a week in the car with my Nono, whom I love but come on—she's my *grandmother*—but on top of that, instead of touring along the coast of California together, just she and I, stopping where we please to take in art, and pedicures, and the occasional great meal or view, we have to go with—ugh—her new husband, Howard "Howie" Howe, which isn't even a name. I mean, did his parents have a stutter? The whole thing is too weird to get used to. My whole life I've had a grandma but never a normal grandpa to match, and that's part of what made

Nono so interesting. She didn't *need* a husband. She didn't *want* a traditional life. And now? That she does? With some hick from Atlanta of all places? A transplant out here who's all *gee-golly* about the weather?

I shudder.

That isn't even the beginning of my troubles, though. Because this isn't simply a trip—it's their *honeymoon*. Who brings their granddaughters along on their honeymoon? It is beyond ick. And why, of all the people I could be stuck with on an old-people honeymoon, does it have to be *her*?

By *her*, I mean Lana. As in, Blah-na. Sure, for about five seconds when I heard about her, when I learned there was for once a cousin my age, I was excited. Maybe I was interested. But the minute we got to the bed-and-breakfast where the wedding was being held, and Mom stopped messing up all my hard work with the straightening iron, I walked around to take in the situation. And saw Lana *in the same dress as me*. Right away, I knew there were going to be problems. Not the least of which being that she was so nerdily excited about it.

"Oh gosh," she said, practically trembling. "I've heard so much about you from Grandma Tess! I've just pictured this moment, and then here we are, standing here, and we have the same outfit!"

Yeah, I thought. *Lucky you.*

I'd picked out the dress on a very bad day. At lunch, Kendra Mack and Cheyenne Taylor had been making fun of the way people laugh, and though they went around the table and did everyone, including themselves, something about the donkey way Kendra Mack made me sound was still sticking in my mind. It made me almost miss Fiona, even though we'll never be friends again after what she did. So that afternoon, when Mom and I went shopping and she badgered me to finally *choose* something already, I grabbed the first dress I saw—all yellows and butterflies. It's way more cutesy than my normal clothes, but it also felt happy in a way I needed, to help make Kendra Mack and her sense of humor bother me less. Don't get me wrong— Kendra Mack is one of my closest friends, and hanging out with her group is a huge step up from being friends with Fiona. I just needed something cheerful that day.

And then, a week later, there's Lana in the same dress. Her hair was in this limp little ponytail, and she was wearing the absolute wrong sandals, gushing away about how crazy it was that her mom had randomly picked this dress out for her—going on about how her mom has no sense of style and never buys her anything cool—and that this obviously meant we were destined to not only be family, but also best friends.

Of course, I was horrified. I told her it was just some

dumb thing my mom made me wear, and that was the end of it. But the rest of the day, Lana kept chattering at my shoulder and would not stop asking me questions. She'd obviously peppered Nono with questions about me too, since she knew *everything*, including embarrassing stories about when I was a baby and visiting some of Nono's commune friends at their hot tub.

She went on and on about my life, my friends, and how much she just loves our grandmother's wild adventures. *My* grandmother, I wanted to correct. Instead I made sure to tell her about the time Nono took me on a special trip to San Francisco when I was nine, just us, to see a ballet and meet her friend who was the choreographer. The way Lana's eyes went wide, and how she started gushing questions again, made it seem even more fabulous than it had felt at the time.

So when, during one of the gross slow dances when the grown-ups were all hanging on each other—Nono and her new husband were practically making out on the dance floor—and Lana asked me if I'd ever been kissed, I smiled in a shy way I'd practiced in the mirror. I told her I'd recently had my first one, with Cory Baxter, at the end-of-the-year dance. I said I'd had a crush on him for a long time and finally got the nerve to tell him about it, even though he's a whole year older. I told her he said he'd always liked me too, and then, under the lights, our lips came together and the whole room swirled and—

It sounded so good it almost felt true.

It wouldn't have been such a big deal if she hadn't kept asking questions, and then swooned about it in front of *Tom*, of all people, as if talking about kissing in front of someone's older brother is ever, ever okay. For the rest of the night, Tom was making kissy faces at me over the shoulders of the aunts and friends of Nono's that his super-charming self had asked to dance. It made me sick, because I knew that wasn't going to be the end of it. Sure enough, soon Dad heard about it. He went straight to Mom, and they both came and informed me I was grounded. Of course I couldn't explain, because then I'd have to confess my lie. That in truth I had never even talked to Cory Baxter for more than three minutes made it even more unbearable. After that I didn't want to *look* at Lana anymore, though everyone kept making us stand together in our matching dresses for pictures.

Ugh. And now I have to be in the car with her. For a week. A whole week away from all my friends, and anything cool that's happening. Luckily, I'll be home in time for Kendra Mack's big end-of-summer pool party, and at least I have my phone with me, so I won't be disastrously out of touch.

Right as I'm tossing the charger into my bag, my brother's nosy face pushes into my room.

"Can't you knock?"

"Mom says to bring your suitcases down. They're almost here. You'll—" He stops short and raises an eyebrow. "Pack enough, Sass? What're they going to do? Strap all that to the roof?" He gawks at the pile by my bed: two suitcases, a cute tote, my purse, and my backpack, which I'm still filling with more shoes, some magazines, and my ceramic-plate hair straightener. "It's only a week. You could dress four people with all this."

"Some people like to wear more than the same nasty T-shirt and shorts for six days in a row," I sneer at him.

"Some people are normal, unlike you," he mutters, taking my heaviest bags, always having to be Mr. Gentleman.

I stick my tongue out like I'm gagging on his smell. It doesn't really take that much imagination. Tom just turned fifteen, and ever since his birthday he coats himself with so much body spray it's like he's a perfume counter saleslady, an image that almost makes me giggle. Maybe Kendra Mack would think that was funny, too. I grab my purse and start digging for my phone to text her about it, but then Mom hollers to say they're here.

"Coming," I groan.

On the stairs, going slow because of both my suitcases,

Tom turns back and gives me one of his evil little grins. "At least you'll come back with lots of great kissing stories from watching Nono and Grandpa Howie."

"Shut up," I grumble, feeling heat rising up in my cheeks. I'm not going to call Nono's husband *grandpa* either, no matter what Tom does or my parents say. But then we're at the landing, and there they all are, standing at the bottom of the stairs in our foyer, looking up at us, beaming.

"Well, you sure are prepared for this," Howie says, trying to be funny. I smile as unenthusiastically as possible without being rude.

"Cassie's favorite way to express herself is through her wardrobe," Nono says admiringly. "It's one of her finest traits."

And that makes me feel good. Nono always understands my enthusiasm for a cute pair of earrings or the perfect scarf. Most of the good accessories I have actually came from her. The pride I feel under her compliment doesn't last long, though, because then Nono says, "And one of Lana's favorite ways of expressing herself is through singing. You should have heard us in the car earlier. It's going to be a great week, joined by such artistic girls."

My eyes meet with Lana's. She's clearly embarrassed, and I'm embarrassed for her. I raise my eyebrows just slightly in *Oh gosh, here we go* sympathy, and the corner of her mouth lifts in enough of a smile to make one of her dimples show. I raise the edge of my own lips back—some kind of pact, maybe, between us. It is, after all, going to be the two of us dealing with the two of them all week.

But then of course she ruins it.

"Your house is so beautiful," she gushes. "You must feel like a princess living here every day."

Ugh. Who wishes they were a princess anymore? Is she five?

"Yeah," I snort, jutting my chin toward my brother, "a princess trapped in a tower with an evil toad."

"Oh, I can't wait for a week without these two at each other," Mom says, coming over to give me a hug. She strokes my hair, which I hate because she always messes it up when she does that. "Have a good time. And listen to your grandparents, okay?"

I nod, turning to Dad and hugging him around the waist. "Don't spend the whole time on your phone, got it?" he says.

"Oh," Howie laughs. "These girls are going to be too busy having real-life fun."

"Good luck with that," Tom mutters, heading out the door to put my suitcases in the car.

And though I hate my brother sometimes for being so

perfect in everyone's eyes and such a jerk when no one sees, this time he's absolutely right. Mom and Dad can make me go on this trip, and they can even make me pretend to like Lana, but there's no way anybody's going to make me have fun.

Chapter Three

Lana

Grandma Tess, Cassie's brother, and her dad arrange and rearrange the bags in the trunk several times, but it's soon clear there's no way everything's going to fit. Mr. Parker tells Cassie she's just going to have to cut her suitcases down to one, and the way she stomps her foot and glares at him before lugging them both back inside is a little alarming. I try to shake off my surprise and listen politely while the grown-ups talk on the lawn, but I really want us to get going. Narrowing things down to a few essential outfits can't be that hard. I'm about to offer to go in and help Cassie when she bangs out of the house again, struggling with her one bulging suitcase even though her brother's trailing behind her, stretching out his hand to help. Her cheeks are flushed and her mouth's set tight, and I think the whole neighborhood must know how mad she is.

Finally, we get in the car and wave to her family. I'm hoping that picking up where we left off at the wedding, only better, will help lift Cassie's mood, but before I can even open my mouth, Grandma Tess asks Cassie how plans are going for her family's Labor Day picnic.

"Fine," is all Cassie says, staring out the window.

I can see our grandmother's brief surprise at such a terse response, but Grandma Tess takes it in stride and breezes on to the next question.

"And tennis camp last week? You enjoyed that coach last year so much. Was she there again?"

"Nope." Cassie's eyes are still fixed on the window, watching the last bits of Monterey disappear behind us. "It was a new coach. I didn't really learn that much."

I want to know more about all this, like how many games has she played and does she win a lot? I wonder if she could teach me, so that we could play together. We have yoga and dance classes at my school, but most of my exercise I get from riding my bike around—I've never taken any kind of sports class or joined any sort of team. Doing something physical that's also a competition sounds like it could be kind of fun. Especially with Cassie.

But what Grandma Tess can't see from the driver's seat,

and I can, is that Cassie doesn't only look uninterested in talking—she looks like she's about to cry. I want to reach out and pat her in some comforting way, but since we didn't even hug at her house, I'm not sure that's a good idea. Right now she clearly needs whatever privacy she can have in a car with three other people.

"So, Grandma Tess," I say, to take the attention off Cassie. "Have you ever gone camping in any of these parks we'll be seeing?"

Grandpa Howe and I have been working together on the plans for this trip, so I know we're going through several incredible national parks and nature reserves in the next eight days. Tonight we're staying at a gorgeous old Spanish ranch that's been converted to a resort-y place with a hotel, spa, and a couple of restaurants—as far from camping as we can get for our first night. Tomorrow we'll go on a tour of a real castle before driving to our next city, where we're taking a class from a famous TV chef who has a fancy bakery there. At least, that's what we're planning, though Grandpa Howe warned me Grandma Tess may get some other last-minute ideas.

"Not down here, Lana." Grandma Tess looks at me through the rearview mirror. "It's part of why I wanted this trip for my honeymoon. Somehow in all my travels, and after living here in California for so long, I've managed not to see much of the country between San Francisco and L.A.—just bopped between them. There was this one time, though, camping in North Carolina—I had joined a few friends during their hike on the Appalachian Trail, taking a break from my dissertation work—"

"There were a lot of those breaks, if I've got the story right," Grandpa Howe says over his shoulder, laughing gently.

Grandma Tess swipes at his leg before going on to tell us about sitting around the campfire with her friends, drinking wine they'd made and singing songs, when they all heard a terrible crashing in the woods that scared them to death.

"You should've seen everyone's faces," she laughs. "Absolutely paralyzed, ears all cocked to the sound. The whole mood went from revelry to sheer terror in two seconds."

I grip Grandpa Howe's headrest to lean forward. "Was it a bear?"

"We thought so. We'd tied up our food the way you're supposed to, but we hadn't been all that careful. None of us could remember what you were supposed to do in a bear attack either. We argued about this for at least an hour the next day on the trail. Were you supposed to get big and loud? Play dead?"

"It's run zigzag downhill, right?" Grandpa Howe says, grinning at Grandma Tess in a way that I know he's teasing. I'm pretty sure big and loud is right, because my best friend, Tamika, knows tons about the wilderness, and I think she's said that before.

Grandma Tess keeps going with the story, mimicking how they all sat there in fear, until her friend jumped up and said she'd rather face whatever it was out there standing.

"We're all about to pee ourselves, with Sally shining her light into the trees. She steps out of the circle—we practically scream for her not to—when she lets out a surprised sound and doubles over in laughter. When she finally pulls herself together, she aims the light back out into the woods to show us what we were all so scared of."

"Jimmy Fallon in a cowgirl costume, right?" Grandpa Howe jokes.

"One of those awful possums!" Grandma Tess says, smacking the steering wheel with the heel of her hand. "We were all quite sure we were about to meet our makers, because of one of those oversized rats." She cracks up.

"Well, that reminds me of a good End of the Road story, actually," Grandpa Howe says. That gets him going on a tale about him and his cousins at their old summer house in Maine, scaring one of Grandpa Howe's big uncles with a mouse. I've heard the story before—Grandpa Howe talks about the End of the Road a lot—but it's a good one. Confident there'll be storytelling for a while now, I sneak a glance at Cassie. When she looks back, she gives me what might be a smile, but then she reaches into her backpack and takes out earbuds. She plugs them in, taps a few times on her phone, and gazes back out the window in her own world with music that she won't share with the rest of us.

This is going to be a very long trip.

Chapter Four

Cassie

We're not even an hour down the road when Nono pulls off the highway. Apparently, a you-pick-them strawberry farm has caught her eye. I haven't been paying attention to much of anything since Lana got Nono and Howie going on their little storytelling contest, but here we are, leaving the exit ramp with Howie pointing the way. Like Nono hasn't navigated all over the world perfectly fine without him all these years.

As we get out, Lana is all smiles, but there's no way I'm getting enthusiastic about some family playdate in a berry patch. The sun is beating down from the cloudless sky, and already I'm hot. These also aren't the right shoes for wandering around in the dirt. I'm stuck in them, though, since I got forced to leave half my wardrobe back home, and there was only room for four pairs.

As Nono and Howie talk to the cheery-faced woman who greets us outside the barn, I text Kendra Mack:

Not even one hour & already it's torture.

Ha poor thing, she types back right away.

Yeah I didn't bring my farmhand outfit for this berry-picking business.

Wear your swimsuit instead!

As if, I type back, following Lana, who's already armed with our two baskets. Howie and Nono have taken off down one of the rows, holding hands and laughing.

I'm typing **Milking goats is probably next** when another text from Kendra Mack comes in: **K! About to see a movie with Izzy Gathing and Gates Morrill, so good luck seeya bye.**

Ugh. Her afternoon sounds so much better than having to watch my favorite grandmother get all smoochy with her new hick husband in the middle of a field. I kick at one of the little plants nearby in frustration, but it only makes a bunch of dirt go up the toe of my sandal.

Lana is half the row ahead of me already, but I can tell she's waiting for me to catch up. I guess I might as well talk to her, since we're stranded out here.

"Is everything okay?" she asks when I get to her.

I squat down, not even sure how to approach a strawberry plant.

"No, everything is not okay. We're baking in the sun, doing manual labor instead of relaxing and having fun, which is what summer's supposed to be *for*, and on top of that my sandals are getting ruined."

"Oh," she says. "I meant, with the texting."

I hand her two berries. "Just a convo with my best friend, Kendra Mack, is all."

Lana adds my strawberries to her basket without looking at them.

"She has two first names?"

So annoying. "No. Mack is her last name."

We pick awhile, not talking, which is nice, until she says, "So, why does she go by both?"

"Because . . ." I scootch down a few more plants. I haven't had to answer this question before. "Because it's cooler. It shows people who you *are*."

I think this is what Kendra Mack would say. At first, when I started hanging with Kendra Mack, it was hard remembering to say "Cheyenne Taylor" or "Izzy Gathing" instead of what I'd been calling them all through sixth grade, but nobody had to *explain* it to me. It's just how it's done.

"So . . ." Lana moves a couple of feet ahead of me. "Is

it like that for everyone at your school? Sounds like it'd be hard to memorize all those first and last names."

"Ugh, no. It's just the people in our group. People who are worth it."

Lana tosses three plump berries into her basket and shifts down the row again. She's taking all the good ones, so I move over to the row next to hers. It will look bad if her basket is brimming and mine isn't even a dozen berries deep.

"Does that mean now I should call you Cassie Parker and you call me Lana Thorton-Howe?"

This is beyond dumb. "Of course not. You're Lana and I'm Cassie and that's it."

"But when I come visit, and we're with your friends, do I say—"

Come visit. As if.

"You know, Lana, you need to learn by observation instead of asking questions all the time. It's classier. And way less annoying. In fact, we're going to need some ground rules if we're going to get through the rest of this trip. Rule Number One is definitely No Annoying Questions, okay?"

"But how do I know they're annoying if I don't ask them?"

I glare at her.

She looks away and moves down another few plants.

"Observation. I get it."

"Rule Number Two is Don't Talk to Me While I Have My Phone. If my phone is in my hand, I'm having a conversation with someone else, not you."

She mutters something, but since she's another ten feet away I don't hear.

"What was that?"

"Nothing."

"Good."

I go back to the plants, checking under leaves and plucking berries even if they're still a little green on top, just so my basket looks fuller. It's not like we're going to be able to eat all these. Probably Nono will take us on another crazy goose chase, looking for a shelter where we can donate them. Ugh. My legs are getting cramped, squatting like this, and I already need a shower. I stand up, stretch, and look across the field where Nono is leaning into Howie as he rubs a bright-red strawberry against her lips before she bites it and kisses him. Gross. I don't even have my sunglasses, and though I brought my phone, I left the earbuds in the car. To make matters worse, Lana's still down there in the dirt, and she's giggling.

"What's so funny?"

"Oh," she gasps, looking a little embarrassed. "I don't know if you'll think it is."

"Oh yeah?"

She looks at me a minute without saying anything, but the edge of her mouth twitches with a smile she's trying to fight.

"I was just thinking, if your friend had a cat or something, would she call it Fluffy Mack? Would your dog be Bow-Wow Parker?"

"I don't have a dog," I tell her, though I can't help giggling. "But our friend Cheyenne Taylor does, and her name is Gypsy."

Lana whistles. "Here, Gypsy Taylor!" she calls in a high voice. "Come on, girl!"

"And Gates Morrill has an iguana he calls Chester."

Lana laughs. "Let me introduce you to my iguana, Chester Morrill."

"And my cockatoo, Bingo McIntosh," I throw in.

"My goldfish, Glub-Glub Peterson."

We're both laughing now.

"My pet rock, Adelaide Beeson."

"Pet rock," she says. "That's a good one."

We make up even more ridiculous names for pets ("Oh, here's my ostrich, Stephanie DiLorio") as we move down our rows together. A breeze kicks up, cooling us even though the sun is warm on our backs. I start to get the hang of squatting and picking. I still don't like being dirty and sweaty, and Lana is still faster than me, but she also has to pause a lot, catching her breath after each giggle breakdown. During one of these, I lean back on my heels to bite into one of my strawberries. There are enough now that it won't hurt eating a few, and I have to admit, the sun-warmed fruit is just the right amount of tart and sweet.

Chapter Five

Lana

fter strawberry picking, the twisty drive along Highway
101 down to Paso Robles is one of the most majestic
things I've ever seen, and we spend the next couple
of hours gasping with astonishment and delight at the view.
There aren't very many places to stop the car and absorb
everything, but Grandma Tess takes the climbing turns
slow, so we can all enjoy as much of the cliffs and crashing
ocean as possible.

By the time we make it into town, we're all breathless
and awed from the natural beauty, but the hotel is almost
just as grand. Grandpa Howe and I picked the fanciest place
we could for our first night's stay, but even after the photos we saw online, I'm still surprised by how beautiful it is

when we pull into the drive. Even Cassie looks impressed as we walk into the lobby, decorated with glossy leather couches and barrel-sized metal vases dripping plants with deep green leaves and tiny magenta flowers all over.

"We thought, for our first night, we ought to do it up right," Grandma Tess says, standing with one hand on Cassie's shoulder and the other on mine.

I know already that Grandma Tess had very rich parents— her trust fund is why she's been able to do whatever she wants since she left home at eighteen, even though she gave a lot of it to charities. But the way she and Grandpa Howe live, you mostly can't tell. Grandpa Howe's been using the same dishware he and Nana Lilia bought together right after they got married, and he probably has some jeans that are about as old. Grandma Tess gives exotic gifts, and has all her travels, but her little cottage with the art studio in the back doesn't look like it came from *Architectural Digest* or anything. So being in a place that is obviously expensive makes me feel a little self-conscious. And grateful.

Grandpa Howe finishes checking us all in, and a valet helps load our bags on a big brass cart to take to our rooms. When he opens the door for me and Cassie, he says, "Misses," and holds out his hand like a prince. We giggle but still go in slowly, both of us checking out the fluffy queen-size beds, the glossy marble in the bathroom, the giant TV, and the vase of bright flowers on the table between the beds.

"We're right across the hall," Grandpa Howe says. It surprises me, but in a good way. If it were Dad and Mom on this trip, we would've had to have the kind of rooms linked by a door. A door you can usually hear everything happening on the other side through, especially a late-night pillow fight.

Grandpa Howe tells us to be ready to head down to the pool in fifteen, and then shuts the door behind him. This room is so beautiful, picking berries with Cassie was so fun, and the drive was so incredible, I feel more relaxed than I have since Mom's headaches started. I flop down on the nearest bed, stretching myself out and making what would be a snow angel in the poufy down comforter.

"Isn't this great?" I say to Cassie, smiling at the ceiling.

"Ugh," she says. "I'm not touching that bed before a shower. I'm filthy."

With that she grabs about three different toiletry bags from her suitcase, plus a handful of bathing suits, before disappearing into the bathroom without asking me whether I need to use it or not.

Suddenly aware of my own dried-sweat T-shirt and still slightly dusty shins and feet, I hop up, pounding the comforter with my palm to bang out any dirt I might've left. Even looking super careful, though, the whole thing is still snowfield white, only a little more lumpy from all my efforts.

I decide it's good that Cassie wanted to go straight into the shower anyway, since I need to call Mom to let her know we're here. I want to see if her voice contains the same tiredness it did this morning. She keeps saying she's just a little "under the weather," and I let her think I believe her because I don't want her to worry about me being worried. But I'm not in fifth grade anymore. That she's trying to hide it means it's really bad. So the more often I can check on her, the better.

She picks up on the second ring, bright and happy. Which makes me miss her in a way I wasn't until just now, but I plunge in and tell her about berry picking, our game of naming pets, and the breathtaking drive above the ocean.

"Oh, I'm so glad you got to see that highway," she says. "It's one of the most beautiful drives I've been on in my life. Your father and I did it when we first got married, and I've always wanted to take you."

A guilty swirl happens in my chest. Mom's always wanted to take me, and now because I've already gone with my grandparents, and she's obviously so sick—no matter what she's pretending—maybe she'll never get to.

I change the subject to chase the bad thought away.

"You should see our hotel, too. There are flowers every-where. What's that kind with the dark glossy leaves and the bright pink—"

"Bougainvillea. Your father loves that stuff. It's very responsive."

"Well, it's everywhere here."

Immediately I miss Dad too—picturing how he'd gaze around that big beautiful lobby with all its arches and terra-cotta tile. My whole chest fills with wanting them both to be here, with me, now. And for nothing bad to be happening. Or for them not to have sent me away while it is.

Getting homesick after not even a day seems babyish even to me, though, so I push all those feelings further down.

"And how's Cassie?" Mom wants to know.

"She's doing great. What about you?" I try to make it sound like I'm just asking because it's what you ask, instead of because I'm worried that any moment she may collapse from exhaustion and stop breathing.

"Oh, it's a busy day, but good," Mom says. "I'll miss you being there when I get home tonight. No freckle-arms to greet me with a hug."

"Well, I'm sending you one right now, then." I close my eyes and squeeze my mom as hard as I can in my mind.

Mom makes an "mmm" sound, and the missing feeling

crashes over me again. I worry my voice will fail when I say, "Miss you, Mom."

"Miss you too. Dad'll be sorry he wasn't here to say hi."

"I'll send him a picture or two of those flowers."

We say our good-byes, and when the call ends, I immediately want to text Dad, but Cassie will be out of that bathroom soon. As far as I know, she hasn't communicated with her parents at all, and I still don't want to look like a baby.

But she doesn't come right out of the bathroom. I can hear her moving around, making little low growls to herself as she does whatever it is she's doing in the mirror, but the door stays shut. Since Grandpa Howe and Grandma Tess will be fetching us any minute, I dig my swimsuit out of my suitcase and change quick, pulling my shorts back on over my suit just as there's a knock at the door.

"Where's Cassie?" Grandma Tess says when she sees me standing there, alone.

"She wanted to shower," I say, hoping that explains it. "And I just called Mom."

"How is she?" Grandma Tess asks.

"Busy," I say, light. "I told her Dad would love all the bougainwhatsit around here."

"It is one of his favorites." Grandpa Howe nods.

"Well, you girls come on down when you're ready,"

Grandma Tess says, putting her hand on Grandpa Howe's tan arm. They both look like they should be on a commercial for a cruise.

"Fancy drinks with umbrellas in them as soon as you get down, okay?" Grandpa Howe adds.

I smile. "We'll be right there."

But we aren't right there. Every time I think Cassie's about to come out of the bathroom, she turns on the hair dryer, runs the water again, or shakes some bottle full of something. Part of me wants to head on down and leave a note that I'll see her at the pool, but I don't want to abandon her and make her come down by herself. Also, while I'm examining everything in the room, I find a card in our bouquet of flowers, which is actually a gift from Grandma Tess. I figure Cassie and I should thank her together.

This only makes me even more eager to get downstairs, though, especially so Grandpa Howe and Grandma Tess won't be wondering where we are. Even though Cassie can't be much longer—we're only going to jump right into the pool, after all, so there's no point in perfect hair—I decide to start a postcard to Tamika, to keep myself from checking the clock every ten seconds. I choose the best one from the batch I bought at the berry farm: a field full of the small leafy strawberry plants under a sunny blue sky.

Tamika would've probably spent more time trying to see how many rows she could leap over than picking, and I like to imagine her in this picture.

> Dear Tamika,
>
> You would've liked our pioneer outing today on the way to Paso Robles. I was all-out Laura Ingalls Wilder bent down in the dirt, and the juicy red sweetness of the strawberries made it extra good. Now we are at this beautiful hotel that's probably too fancy for cowgirling, but I'll see what I can do. Cassie and I are—

I'm about to write "getting along great," because that seems mainly true, though it has been a rockier start than I wanted. Tamika doesn't have a lot of patience for wishy-washiness in the emotional department, so "great" would do fine, but I end up not writing anything, because finally the bathroom door opens. Cassie's there, looking like she's about to go to a poolside *ball* instead of just hang out with me and our grandparents.

"I didn't think you were still here," she says. I can't tell if she's embarrassed to have taken so long, or disappointed she has to make her appearance with me.

"I wanted some solo time too," I say back.

"Are they down there already?"

"They're waiting, yeah. Grandpa Howe said he'd get us fancy drinks."

Cassie's bending to put her dirty clothes from this morning into some kind of clear plastic zip-up bag, so it seems at first that maybe she's miffed about the idea, but when she stands back up, she's smiling.

"Well, let's make sure they're as fancy as this room is, then."

Chapter Six

Cassie

've got to hand it to Nono and Howie—they picked a stunning hotel for our first night. The whole place is posh, and I love all the organic shampoo and lotions in the bathroom. The pool is even more spectacular. Glowing lanterns are strung above the patio, with a few threaded over the water so their light glimmers on its surface. There are waiters in crisp shirts, and lounge chairs with striped cushions as thick as the mattress on Tom's futon. There's a cabana bar along the right side of the pool, where women in stylish cover-ups sip icy drinks and smile at each other or their handsome companions.

"Kendra Mack would die," I whisper, reaching into my bag to get my phone for a picture.

"There's Grandma Tess and Grandpa Howe," Lana says, pointing. I press her arm down with my hand and whisper through the side of my teeth: "Rule Number Three: No Pointing, Ever." Part of it's because pointing is rude, but also because I've spotted some good-looking teenage boys hanging out together on the opposite side of the pool. I don't know if they've seen us yet—I hope not, since I had to come in next to Lana and her mighty Speedo one-piece—but I don't want to make them think Lana and I are talking about them, either.

"Well, I hope the photo turns out," she says. "I'm getting in."

I drift over to the curved corner of the pool, where there are some empty tables with bronze umbrellas over them. I'm taking photos, while also sneaking glances at the boys, trying to get a sense of how old they are.

I send Kendra Mack the best one of the pool, with the message **Cute boys here too!**

This gets her attention. **As cute as Loverboy?**

I blush and can't help smiling. Ever since my former best friend Fiona's Big Horrible Diary Betrayal, I haven't talked to *anyone* about my secret crush on Cory Baxter, unless you count telling Lana he was my boyfriend. But Kendra Mack needs info on everyone, and doesn't seem to let up, ever, so she's always trying to get me to spill about who it is I like. Cory Baxter isn't really the kind of boy Kendra Mack and her friends think of in a romantic way, though. Eventually I'll tell her, of course. I just want to make sure the other girls won't think I'm lame for liking him. Or that Kendra Mack won't forbid me to stop, like she did one time to Neftali Manji when she said a boy in the grade below us was cute. It's a fun game between me and Kendra Mack, anyway—her making a big deal about my secret Loverboy.

Just as cute, I type back, shooting a glance at the boys. **But sportier.**

Ooh, ooh. You should invite them to your Labor Day party.

I pause. My family throws a barbecue in the backyard every Labor Day weekend, but it's not like a big party. Mom and Dad invite their best couple friends over, and Tom and I are allowed to invite one or two friends as well. We eat a lot of grilled food, play badminton, and run around with sparklers. This year, since Fiona and I aren't friends anymore, I mentioned it to Kendra Mack, which brought on a ton of questions about what she should wear, and who would be there. Whether Tom was inviting any high school friends. It seems like she thinks it's a lot fancier than it really is.

Your pool party is sooner. Should I invite them to that? I type.

45

Only if they're REALLY cute. Send a pic!

Getting close enough to catch a picture of the boys makes me nervous, but if Kendra Mack asks you to do something, you don't chicken out. So I stroll leisurely around the opposite side of the pool to find a good shot, passing Lana and our grandparents crowded together on one of those giant lounge floats. Nono and Howie already have fruity drinks, but Lana must be waiting for me before she gets hers.

"Hey, you guys look great," I holler, positioning myself so that the cute boys are right behind them. "Let me take your picture."

"Come get in the pool, Cass." Nono paddles them closer. "We miss you."

"Right there is good," I say, not wanting her to mess up my shot. "It looks so pretty with the light. Say cheese."

They smile and I click my screen. Then I tilt it just a little higher to catch the boys, so jittery I think I might drop my phone in the water.

"I'll get in in a minute," I call back to them, crossing back over to my table.

The picture isn't very good, but I send it to Kendra Mack anyway.

Not bad, not bad. Are you going to talk to them? she texts back.

No way. Not in front of my grandparents, anyway.

Oh yeah. They grossing you out yet?

Since they've brought us to such a knockout place, and really haven't been that bad so far, except for the strawberry patch gooeyness, I don't want to talk bad about Howie and Nono.

No vomiting yet. Now, my stepcousin, on the other hand . . .

I can imagine.

Kendra Mack knows all about Lana—at least the annoying parts. Lana's utter cluelessness delighted the whole lunch table when I told them about her after the wedding, so I amped up her dorkiness and all the questions she kept asking. (Though of course I skipped over the ones about me and the wish-it-happened kiss with Cory Baxter.) I also left out how I got in trouble, and Lana's dead-on impression of the crazy, champagne-silly great-aunt who kept pulling everyone onto the dance floor.

Yeah, well. I'm stuck for now, I guess, I type. **So glad we'll be able to celebrate my freedom at your party!**

Another text comes in while I'm typing: one from Izzy Gathing. It's a thrill and a surprise, since Izzy Gathing is second-best friends with Kendra Mack. (Cheyenne Taylor is first, and Neftali Manji is third, which means I'm fourth if you don't count Gates Morrill.) Even after all my time at the lunch table, Izzy Gathing has never gotten super friendly with me, so to hear from her now almost makes me squeal.

KM is finalizing invitations and wants to know if there's anyone else you think she should invite?

That Izzy's asking me is too exciting to question. I make a couple of safe suggestions—people I'm pretty sure Kendra Mack's already invited but that will be cool and thoughtful for me to mention. I wish I could throw in Cory Baxter's name casually, but if I'm not telling Kendra Mack about him yet, I'm certainly not telling Izzy Gathing.

While I'm doing that, another text comes in from Kendra Mack: **Cheyenne Taylor's here, so I have to go. We're planning outfits. Have you thought about what you're wearing?**

While I finish typing to Izzy Gathing, and start replying to Kendra Mack, I see Lana coming my way. Probably sent over by Nono.

I'm going shopping this week too! I lie. Souvenir shops are probably the closest thing to a mall I'll see all week, even though shopping used to be one of Nono's and my favorite things. Before Howie and Lana came along.

I catch Kendra Mack's last message right as Lana reaches my table: **Awesome. Send more pics! ;)**

Lana is clearly not happy to have been sent on this

mission. "Grandpa Howe wants to know if you're ready for your poolside beverage, since you're not coming over."

"I was just finishing up," I say, lifting my hair to let it spill down over my shoulder in a way I know looks regal.

"Okay, well. I'm going over to the cabana to order."

I put my phone away and sneak a glance at the boys' side of the pool. They're definitely looking over here now.

"I'll go with you," I say, smiling wide and letting Lana go ahead. It's a trick Cheyenne Taylor does, to make sure any boys watching will see her walking away.

Chapter Seven

Lana

When Cassie finally puts her phone back, I notice that her cute little beaded bag matches her swimsuit in the most perfect way. I want to ask her where she got it, but Rule Number One: No Annoying Questions is sticking in my head, so I say nothing. At the cabana, the guy behind the bar asks us what he can do for us, and Cassie pores over the menu with this look on her face that I guess she thinks is aloof, but I already studied the drinks list while Grandpa Howe and Grandma Tess were ordering theirs, so I'm ready.

"Kids' Banana Colada, please," I say, smiling as nice as I can.

Cassie tosses her hair and acts like she can't decide.

"What do you think is best?" she asks the guy serving us.

"Well, it depends," he says, amused. "What sort of thing are you in the mood for? Creamy and sweet? Maybe something tart, like strawberry?"

Cassie glances at me. We both smile. "I think I've had enough strawberry today."

"How about a Blue Lagoon, then?" he says, making Cassie blush for some reason. "It's blue raspberry, coconut milk, and pineapple—very refreshing."

"That sounds perfect," she says.

We watch the pool while we wait for our drinks. It looks like Cassie and I are maybe the youngest people here, though I see a group of teenage boys pushing each other around in the deep end.

"They are soooo cute," Cassie says.

I look again. They seem more like horsey goofballs to me, but if Cassie thinks they're cute, then they must be, since she knows so much more about that kind of stuff than I do.

"Let's go closer when our drinks are ready and see if they talk to us," she says.

The Annoying Question comes out of my mouth before I can stop it: "But what about your boyfriend?"

She blushes again, this time not as prettily as she did

when she ordered her drink. "It'd just be talking. Don't you think it'd be fun?"

Mostly I want us to be together with no one else around, but it doesn't seem Cassie's so into that, and if she won't let me ask her questions, I'm not sure how much talking can get done, anyway.

So as the waiter delivers our drinks—Cassie's is as blue as a Smurf and mine has a huge skewer of bananas and pineapple poking out the top, plus the tropical umbrellas as Grandpa Howe promised—I mask my disappointment and say, "Sure." She positions us across from the boys, and we sit on the edge with our legs in the water.

Cassie leans back on one hand and takes a sip from her drink. "So, who do you like back home?"

I think of Tamika, and Grandpa Howe and Grandma Tess, of course, plus the grown-up friends I have because of Mom and Dad, but that isn't what Cassie means.

"Well, I have this friend Henry," I try.

Cassie's eyes get curious for the first time on this trip. "What's he like?"

"Um, he's got brown hair, and brown eyes. He likes mountain biking a lot. . . ."

Suddenly she's the one with Annoying Questions: "How do you know him? Do you see each other a lot? Is he cute?"

I try to remember how Henry and I started being friends. "We have art class together. And sometimes we ride bikes on the weekend, around the park near where we live." I avoid the cute question altogether.

"So, like, a date?"

I think about this. Henry lives on the other side of the park from me. Usually we meet in the middle and ride around whatever trails we feel like until we're ready to go home. Sometimes we talk, but mostly to point out birds or people or interesting growths on trees. I like being with Henry because he's someone my age but isn't as busy and loud as Tamika and her brothers can be. There are never parents around when we go on our rides, but I don't think anyone would consider them dates. With Cassie looking at me like that, though, I wonder if that's what Henry thinks they are. I'm not sure I'd like it as much if he did.

"No, they're not dates," I finally say.

"Well, do you like him, though?"

I picture Henry in my mind: his puzzled concentration when we stumble on a plant he hasn't seen before. The way he can spot birds high up in trees that no one would ever notice. The navy-striped Keds he wears, and how good he is with watercolors. Probably somebody likes Henry in a crushing way, but it's not me.

"He's my friend. It's hard to see him in, you know, that

way." I gesture faintly to the high school boys, then stop myself, remembering the No Pointing rule. They've gotten out of the water and are digging into a big plate of nachos their mom ordered, so they probably wouldn't notice, but Cassie would.

"Well, I bet he likes you, if he's constantly asking you out for bike rides," she says.

"I don't think that always has to be true." It comes out in an abrupt way that surprises me. When Cassie's face shows the same surprise, I apologize and take a sip of my drink, hoping it counts as a way of changing the topic.

"Don't be sorry," she says back. "I'm just curious what you mean."

I look at her. I haven't really thought about this much, but I try to explain.

"I just don't think a boy has to be in love with you to spend time with you. In fact, it's nicer if he isn't, right? Then you can have fun without all that weird stuff. You can hang out without constantly thinking about holding hands." It's embarrassing to say that, but I don't pause. "That seems like it would be sad."

Cassie's looking at me with an expression that's part processing what I've said, part agreeing, part not sure. I'm not sure either, since I don't usually talk about boys and crushes, especially not with someone like Cassie.

"I haven't ever thought about it like that," she says, looking back across the water, though not at the boys. "But I think you're right."

A wave of relief, and pleasure, spreads over me. "I guess all your friends at home have boyfriends, though, huh?"

Cassie makes an annoyed snort. "Not everybody. Kendra Mack and Cheyenne Taylor always have boys they're crushing on, but that never lasts for long. Maybe, like, one day. Two class periods, sometimes."

"That sounds hard to keep up with."

"It is," she says, rolling her eyes at first but then straightening up. "I mean, that's just because Kendra Mack has such high standards."

I can tell she doesn't want to talk badly about her friends, so I change the subject.

"She must approve of you and Cory together, though, right?"

Cassie blinks and takes a long sip of her drink. "Sure. She thinks he's terrific."

I ask her about what group dates they've gone on together, but she tells me she and Cory don't see each other a lot because they don't share any classes and her parents are so strict.

"He'll be at Kendra Mack's pool party when we get back, though," she says with a far-off smile.

I want to ask her more, but the boys from the other side of the pool have finished their nachos and decide to take that exact moment to leap into the water not far from us. Their giant splash soaks us both.

"Oh my god," Cassie says, pushing back her half-wet hair. "Do you think they did that on purpose?" She sounds aggravated but also a little delighted.

I shrug. I'm not sure what their jumping in the pool would have to do with us, or why it would be a good thing if it did. Mainly, I think it was funny, but I can't tell if that's okay or not.

Cassie squeezes out the ends of her hair. "Think we can make a bigger splash?" she asks.

I smile back at her. "We at least need to try."

Chapter Eight

Cassie

Being at the pool with Lana was more fun than I expected. I thought what she said about sometimes boys being better as friends was interesting, though Kendra Mack and Cheyenne Taylor certainly wouldn't agree. Lana reminds me a little of the way Fiona used to be, actually, though Lana's a lot quirkier around the edges. Still, I let myself envision some never-going-to-happen alterna-world where Fiona and I are friends again, and I get to introduce the two of them to each other. It almost feels nice.

Once we're back in the room, I hit the bathroom to redo my hair and makeup. As I stand there with the blow-dryer, I almost wish I could tell Lana the truth about Cory

Baxter. Or at least say we broke up after the wedding, so I wouldn't have to keep lying to her. Since I said that thing about him being at Kendra Mack's pool party, though, I guess it's too late. Besides, even though Cory hardly knows who I am, I can't stand the idea of us breaking up, even in my head. He's an impossible fantasy for me, but in Lana's eyes Cory's my boyfriend, and in spite of being complicated, it's strangely pleasant to pretend with her it's true.

I'm pulled from my dreaming two steps out of the bathroom when Lana bolts past and slams the door without even an "Excuse me." For a second I feel bad about making her wait so long, but then I see what she's done to the room. Her duffel bag gapes open on the armchair in the corner, and somehow she's spilled half her belongings onto the floor next to it. The desk is cluttered with her phone, room key, some tissues, a bunch of change, a Chap-Stick, two smashed strawberry blossoms, some pebbles she must've picked up at the farm, a watch I hadn't even noticed she was wearing, and about seven gum wrappers. On top of that are a scattering of postcards, three pens, and a sheet of stamps. In a matter of forty-five minutes she's managed to *destroy* our room. Unbelievable.

She also apparently showers faster than anyone I know, because I haven't even changed out of my robe before she's stepping out in a pair of clean jeans and a ruffly green top that's actually cute. I'm about to tell her so when I see into the bathroom, where she's flung her towel thoughtlessly over the shower rod, the mat is still on the floor instead of hung back over the tub edge, her swimsuit is dripping off the towel rack, and everything on the sink has gotten moved out of place. Ugh.

Calmly and deliberately I select my dinner outfit, making a point of zipping my suitcase back up and putting it in our giant closet. I turn on the light inside and shut the door behind me. I'd rather change in the closet than go back in that hideous bathroom.

Lana's typing something into her phone when I come out, but as soon as she hears me she puts it back on the desk, facedown.

"You ready?" she says, trying to be casual, though I can tell she's irritated for some reason. Like she has any reason to be irritated with me.

I'm looking even less forward to Howie's stories and jokes at dinner if Lana's going to be in a snit, but back in the company of our grandparents, she's fine. Our reservations are at the fancy restaurant in the converted barn on the hotel grounds, which is a short walk through a vineyard. The sun is setting, and the sky is a beautiful salmon streak of pink. Howie and Lana hold hands and walk together down the path. Nono falls into step with me behind them, and thoughts of Lana and everything else wash away. I finally have my Nono alone.

"I'm so glad you're here," she says, linking her arm with mine. "I didn't get to go on these kinds of adventures until I was—well, much older."

"Why not?" I ask.

She pushes back her hair, making her wavy silver bob even prettier. "My parents were much more traditional and strict. In their world, there were things that proper people did, and things they didn't. Especially girls. It wasn't until I was sixteen that I realized there might be other ways of living. But I also understood I might have to do them without the family I was born to."

"Was it on that trip with your mom?" I know that Nono, her sister, and my great-grandmother all went on a trip to Europe when Nono was sixteen and Aunt Jackie was eighteen. Nono's talked about wanting to take Tom and me on a similar trip one day, "though with much more fun in it."

She looks at me thoughtfully. "It was, actually. Or rather, right after that."

"What happened?"

"A lot of things, I guess."

I watch her face—how the taffy light makes her skin and eyes glow, even though she sounds a little sad.

"During the whole trip there were places outside our guided tour that I wanted to go," she tells me. "I wanted to explore more of the neighborhoods—meet the real people, experience their food and music—but Mother felt it wasn't appropriate for us to wander. She wanted us to be 'cultured' but was appalled by anything outside of what might be societally appropriate. Which meant, anything that wasn't exactly like her. I got in a huge fight with Jackie about it when she took Mother's side. Her response shocked me.

"I was given the whole lecture about the proper behavior for young ladies again and again. The same came from Father when we got home, only worse. I wasn't allowed to attend events without Mother or Jacqueline after that."

I try to imagine Nono doing anything "proper" and can't.

"So that's when you left?"

"I had to finish high school first. Up until the very day I received that diploma I played the role they wanted, though after that trip I knew no one was going to keep me from going on adventures and talking with all kinds of people in all kinds of places. Not even my beloved sister. It was a very difficult time for us for a long while."

It's as hard for me to imagine Nono and Aunt Jackie fighting as it is imagining Nono being proper. They seem like the best of friends. "How come?"

"Probably because I wanted to be me and she wanted me to be her, and we both wanted the other to be more the same. Once we started focusing on our differences, they were all we could see, for longer than either of us liked."

It's not exactly the same situation, but Fiona pops into my mind again. Even before the Diary Incident, we'd both gotten interested in different things.

"We got over it, eventually," Nono goes on. "You do with the people you really love. When we came back home, though, I knew I couldn't survive the limited life my family had in mind for me and started widening my horizons. Sneaking to cafés and poetry readings, meeting new people. Hearing a friend's stories about California and the communal life there is what eventually got me on a bus out West."

"I'm glad you did," I say, squeezing Nono around the waist. There's more to say, maybe, but we've arrived at the barn.

Nono squeezes me back. "I am too."

As soon as we're seated at the table, Lana and Howie immediately flip to the backs of their menus, oohing and aahing about chocolate mousse, caramel custard, and apple-praline tart. I can't help wishing they weren't here and that this trip was one whole adventure Nono and I could have to ourselves.

"They like to eat dessert first," Nono tells me, grinning.

"Well," I say, stiffening my spine, "I plan on eating like a normal person."

"Suit yourself," Nono says before choosing the house-made lemon sorbet.

I have to lift my menu up high so Lana and Howie won't see me glowering at them behind it.

Chapter Nine

Lana

Even though Grandma Tess said at dinner last night that we don't need to meet for breakfast this morning until nine, Cassie's alarm blares off at seven a.m., like it would if we were in school. I ignore it as best I can and burrow deeper into my pile of fluffy pillows while she tiptoes into the bathroom.

The next time I open my eyes it's 7:34. Cassie is still in the shower. I lie in the big bed awhile, wondering what kind of mood she's going to be in when she comes out. When we got back to the room after dinner, all Cassie wanted to do was get in her pajamas and watch TV. I had really been looking forward to sharing more secrets, but I guessed we still had all week for that. Even though I didn't really know any of the characters on her show, it did end up being funny, and on top of laughing with her, it felt really good to have a cousin who could help me learn about all the coolest things for once.

I just wish she weren't so unpredictable. And such a bathroom hog. I don't think I could spend that much time getting ready in the morning even if I was Marie Antoinette.

Right now, though, I really need to get in there myself, and it isn't for my hair. Probably I should just knock, but somehow I'm afraid Cassie'll come up with some other rule if I don't wait for her to finish. As a distraction, I pick my outfit for the day, but dressing only takes about two minutes. Like yesterday, I keep thinking she's going to come out any second, and that makes my need to go even worse.

I move to the desk and pick up my phone, perching in the leather-seated chair and crossing my legs, tight. I know if I call Mom or Dad it might be hard to disconnect as soon as Cassie's done, so I text them instead, saying good morning and that I'll call them later in the afternoon. Almost immediately two chimes ring in, both of them wishing me a happy day, but I don't read on, because the bathroom door finally opens. I dash past Cassie to take care of my business, mad and embarrassed that this is the second time this has happened, but not sure what to do about it.

Cassie's full-on scowling when I come out. Her bed is made as perfectly as it was when we first arrived, and she's sitting on its edge, changing things from that beaded purse I liked last night into a sturdier leather one with a buckled strap. More like she's slinging things from one purse to another, making frustrated little sighs as she does it.

I wait to see if she'll say anything, but then finally I just ask, "What's the matter?" Annoying Question or not, I'd rather not have to guess.

"You have to ask me?" She holds her hands out to encompass the room.

I look around. The room is gorgeous, and luxurious—even better with the morning sunshine pouring in. The flowers from Grandma Tess are so pretty, and—

"This room is a pigsty," she says. "Staying with you is worse than staying with my brother."

Hot shame shoots into my cheeks, making me snap without thinking. "I'd rather live with a messy roommate than one who hogs the bathroom all morning and doesn't seem to care what anyone else out here might need."

Cassie squares her shoulders. "I get up early so that you can sleep later while I get ready. If you think about it, it's me being more polite. And besides, if you really need to go, you can knock. If you're too timid to ask for what you need, that's not my fault."

That Cassie's using the same calm, talking-down tone Mom gets when she's mad only makes it burn even more. "It *is* your fault if you can't think about anyone but yourself all the time," I say.

Her coolness suddenly evaporates. "I'll spell it out for you, then, since you can't grasp the basics on your own: Rule Number Four? Knock If You Need To!"

I try to copy Cassie's mean tone to hide how shaky I feel. "Fine, I'll knock. And I'll be neater with my things if it bothers you so much."

She snorts and rolls her eyes. "Like you'd know how."

It disappoints me to the core that we're fighting after not even a whole day. But more than being disappointed, I'm also mad.

"You can hate me for saying so if you want to, Cassie, but you're not the only one on this trip." Confronting her is scary, but I keep my voice strong. "Grandma Tess and Grandpa Howe will be here for breakfast in about three seconds, and we need to make their trip nice. You may not like me very much, but Rule Number Five needs to be: In Front of the Grandparents, We Act Like Friends."

She's not looking at me, only staring into both her purses to make sure everything's been transferred from one to the other. Finally she leans back on her hands, looks at the ceiling, and says, "Fine."

I wait for her to say something more and also for my heart to calm down, but she sits there, doing nothing, all the way until my pulse is a little more normal.

"Good, then," I say finally.

I turn my back to her and pull the sheets and covers up on my bed. I straighten the comforter and each pillow just so, even though we're checking out, and someone will be changing the sheets anyway. I do it as fussily as I can, and almost make myself laugh with the prissy look I put on my face. Fortunately, right then there's a knock at the door and Grandma Tess chirps, "Good morning!"

Without acknowledging each other in any way, Cassie and I singsong, in perfect harmony, "Good morning!" right back.

Chapter Ten

Cassie

When we sit down to breakfast at the hotel restaurant, I can barely look at Lana. She and Howie start right off with the jokes, debating whether doughnuts or chocolate éclairs really count as dessert, or if they should ask the waiter for ice cream instead. I'm halfway through an eye roll—they can't really mean to have dessert before breakfast?—when Lana kicks me under the table. It surprises me so much I exclaim aloud, and Lana gives me a look that's almost as harsh as one of Izzy Gathing's. It's shocking, this side of Lana, and almost impressive. I suppose if I want her to keep following my rules, it's only fair to follow hers, so I throw in that I think doughnuts count as cake even if they're a breakfast food. Howie orders a plate of them for the table, before we consider anything else.

It's probably too early for Kendra Mack to be awake yet, but as soon as we're headed out to the car with our suitcases, I check my phone anyway.

"What is it that's so important, Cassie?" Nono says with a hint of irritation. "It's like you're attached to that thing."

"My friend back home is planning a party and needs help is all," I say, sliding my phone back into my purse. I knew this trip was going to be horrible.

"Speaking of parties," Howie says as he gets in the front seat, "this place we're visiting today had world-famous ones. It'll be great to see the rooms up close instead of simply in photos, though those are impressive themselves. Did Lana tell you anything about it, Cassie? As soon as we saw the website, we knew we had to take you there. I have a feeling you'll want to move in."

It's all I can do not to roll my eyes. Like he and Lana would know anything about what I like. Or where I'd want to live.

"I know going to the house of some newspaperman sounds boring," Lana chirps to me as we buckle up, "but Hearst Castle looks incredible. It has Egyptian artifacts, a private zoo, sixty bedrooms, and two swimming pools!"

Ugh. Someone has got to tell Lana how uncool it is, getting so worked up about things. But Nono's nodding along, looking equally into this castle idea, and when Nono wants to try something, it's usually pretty fun. I decide maybe she and I can lose Lana and Howie in one of the sixty bedrooms. But not before showing Lana how good I can be at Rule Number Five.

"Oh, I think it sounds great, Lana," I say as brightly as I can. "What a beautiful and educational idea for us."

Neither Nono nor Howie see us shooting I Can't Stand You faces at each other across the backseat.

It's harder to be mad at Lana when we get there. I thought she was being overly excited, but the whole place is absolutely stunning. Eighteen times bigger and prettier than our hotel. I take ten photos at the front entrance, sending some to Kendra Mack. I'm tempted to mention to her how great it would be to have a party here, but I don't want to sound too Lana-ish about it. Still, it's fun to imagine myself walking down that staircase in a sparkly gown.

"Gorgeous already, right?" Howie tries to look over my shoulder at the photos, but I move my screen so he can't.

He acts like he doesn't notice. "Speaking of gorgeous, I haven't gotten a picture of you three girls together yet," he says, unzipping that dorky camera case he wears around his neck. "How about over there, by the lion."

Nono moves in front of a giant black marble lion statue

71

and puts her arm around Lana. I don't want my picture taken with Lana right now, especially since she's getting cutesy with my grandmother, but Nono reaches out for me to join them under her other arm. As Howie tells us to smile, I hear Lana whisper, "I'd like you to meet my marble lion, Josh Pepperkinickey."

And I can't stop the giggle that comes out my nose as Howie clicks the shutter.

Though Hearst Castle is interesting, our tour guide certainly isn't. He's some old red-faced guy with a hooked nose and drone-on voice. Thank goodness as soon as the tour starts up, my phone chirps in a message so I don't have to listen too long.

Yup. Been there. That place is cool, Kendra Mack has responded, obviously not impressed. Of course Kendra Mack has been here before. I ask back which tour she took.

Oh, we didn't stay long.

Well, you missed out, I type, remembering the boys at the pool yesterday and how they got Kendra Mack's attention. **The tour guide is better-looking than the rest of it!**

Sounds like Loverboy's going to be replaced. Poor thing. Do you think Cheyenne Taylor will snap him up next?

I smile and laugh a little. Cheyenne Taylor might agree

Cory Baxter's good-looking, but she doesn't go for boys who are shorter than she is. Or who like video games and science fiction more than soccer.

"You telling Kendra Mack she should move her pool party to this place?" Lana says, appearing next to me, all friendly. Like we weren't fighting five minutes ago.

I tuck my phone back in my purse without responding to Kendra Mack. It's cooler not to answer that kind of question, anyway.

"You're right that it's pretty." I shrug, still not sure if I should let Lana off the hook.

"The Hearsts were one of the richest families in America," she says, like she's the tour guide now. "Their daughter, Patty, lived here like this total princess but turned into some kind of rebel terrorist and bank robber later on. Isn't that crazy?"

"You've got to stop saying 'princess' like that, Lana," I tell her. Though the rebel-terrorist-bank-robber thing sounds potentially cool.

"Well, I don't know what else to call it when the name of her house includes the word 'castle.'"

She doesn't know it, but that was a pretty good comeback.

"Probably had a bunch of servants too, I guess," I say as we follow the tour group into the enormous dining room.

It's hung with old tapestries. At the center is a table with at least ten chairs on each side.

Her eyebrows go up. "I know. Can you imagine what it would take to run a place like this? Or to clean it?"

I fake shudder. "Not if you were living here, no."

She blushes but smiles back. The group moves out to what our guide announces is the Neptune Pool, and we both gasp at the same time. There are giant marble statues all around the flawless pool, with a massive Roman-looking building complete with columns and reclining figures standing at one end.

"Oh, I wish Tamika could see this," Lana breathes next to me.

"Who's Tamika?"

"My best friend. Although—" She pauses, and the hesitant look on her face makes me curious.

"Although what?"

"I just mean that Tamika's probably not the same kind of best friend Kendra Mack is, is all."

I stiffen a little. "What do you mean?"

"I mean, Tamika is fantastic. She's the most athletic person I know, even though she isn't on a team or anything. She can beat all three of her brothers in a wrestling match. She knows everything you'd want to know about women explorers and politicians, and she can hit the *O* in a can of SpaghettiOs with a pellet gun from fifty feet. She also comes up with amazing games. And she sews."

I realize Lana's doing that thing that *I* do when Kendra Mack asks me what I think about someone: super highlight even the tiniest good points so that you don't say anything bad, in case she goes behind your back and tells them about it. But I like Lana better when she's says things straight out. Even, I realize, when she's mad.

"So where's the but?" I push her.

"Oh, there's no but, really. Like I said, Tamika's my best friend."

I raise my eyebrows.

"It's just that it seems like you and Kendra Mack are really tight. You know, talking and texting all the time, telling each other everything."

I make a noncommittal "mmm" to get her to go on.

"And, well, Tamika and I come up with all kinds of games, and her house is really loud and fun and I love hanging out with her, but we don't really, you know, *talk*."

It might be because I have to squint in the sun, but when Lana says that last part, it seems a cloud of disappointment crosses her face.

"So, what kinds of things do you do, then?" I find it hard to imagine what else you'd do with a best friend. Even Fiona and I spent most of our time together talking.

We trail behind the tour through more rooms and halls, and Lana's face lights up as she tells me about the Olympics she and Tamika plan every year. How they're always finding new places in the woods at the park, coming up with wilderness adventures, putting on plays they write together, or going off road on their bikes. None of that is really my thing, but Lana makes it sound exciting in the same way I've overheard Cory make his video games sound exciting with his friends. I feel a little bad that all my texting with Kendra Mack seems to make Lana compare her to *her* best friend.

"Tamika sounds cool," I say, because she does. Not the Kendra Mack kind of cool, but still—interesting and fun. I almost tell Lana that Tamika might be someone my old best friend Fiona would like too, but I swallow it. Who cares who Fiona would like?

We peek into the next big room: a real movie theater with deep red walls, a small stage with a screen standing over it, and carved gold statues holding electric lights.

"Oh gosh, I have to get a picture." Lana takes out her phone. "Tamika would love this."

"Here, use my camera instead." I fish out the little Canon I brought with me. "It takes better ones than a phone."

She smiles. "Thanks."

I tell her which settings to use in this light, and how to zoom closer when the ones she takes are too blurry.

The tour ends back in the massive Assembly Room, where the grown-ups are offered glasses of champagne. While Nono and Howie chat with the other guests, Lana and I keep taking pictures of each other, posing as though we're here for an old-world glamorous party. It's silly but fun, and Lana has some great suggestions for dramatic poses. I say I'll be sure to send copies to her later, though I'll probably delete them all way before we get home.

Chapter Eleven

Lana

After Hearst Castle, we head south to Visalia. There isn't time for any crazy stops, because we want to make it to the baking demo class we're taking this afternoon with TV celebrity chef Brick Hasselback. Grandpa Howe has watched his cupcake challenge show for over a year, and he can't wait to learn the secrets of buttercream icing from a pro. We had to sign up weeks and weeks ago to make sure all four of us could get in, and if we don't arrive in time, we forfeit our spaces.

We do have time to stop for lunch at least, and while Cassie and I are washing up in the bathroom, I try to get our conversation from the castle going again.

"How long have you and Kendra Mack been friends?" I ask.

"We ride the same bus," she says quick, taking out her phone because a text has come in.

I watch a minute while she types. "Since elementary school?"

"Since sixth grade. We didn't start hanging out until this spring, though." She puts her phone on the edge of the sink and checks herself in the mirror, but it chimes again right away. This time when she looks at it, she rolls her eyes.

"Cheyenne Taylor's asking if I want to play tennis this afternoon. It's sweet"—she types a quick response and then digs in her purse for some lip gloss—"but Cheyenne Taylor is also kind of stupid. She knows I'm on this trip. I whined to everyone about a hundred times. Though maybe she's just trying to rub it in my face that I'm not there with the rest of them."

If you ask me, Cassie's friends sometimes sound a little more like enemies. I wonder why she doesn't hang out with more thoughtful people.

"Who was your best friend before Kendra Mack?" I ask, hoping I'm not in No Annoying Questions territory.

Fortunately, Cassie forgets the rule, or is too distracted

by her reflection to care. "Just this lame girl. Kendra Mack helped me realize that she wasn't a very good friend."

"Oh. What did she do?"

Cassie turns to face me with such intensity I worry for a second she's angry with *me*. "She betrayed my trust. She was careless with my secrets. She humiliated me, and she never even said 'I'm sorry.'"

She tosses her hair a final time in the mirror. "But I'm glad that all happened, because Kendra Mack is fabulous. Being her friend is fabulous, and now my life is fabulous. I don't even think about Fiona anymore. Like, ever. Okay?"

I swallow, startled by the sudden ferocity of Cassie's voice. "Okay."

Back at the table, Grandma Tess is laughing at something Grandpa Howe just told her while they were waiting for us, and their smiles put one on my face, too.

"Hilarious," Cassie mutters.

"Oh, it is," Grandma Tess says back, either not noticing Cassie's grouchiness or ignoring it. "Tell them, Howie."

"Oh, I was just saying that you could've fit the entire house at the End of the Road in about one of those rooms we saw today."

Between ordering our food and eating, Grandpa Howe explains to Cassie how his grandfather built the old summer cabin in Maine. While he's talking, another message comes in on Cassie's phone, and when she starts to reach for it, Grandma Tess gives her a disapproving look. Cassie sees it, puts on an I'm Totally Listening face, and straightens up. Grandpa Howe hasn't skipped a beat, telling us how one summer his own father tried following in his dad's footsteps by expanding the back porch all by himself.

"Every day that month, Mother would send my brothers and me out on longer and longer hikes, telling us not to come back until we'd found, well, all kinds of crazy things. An old snake's skin. A certain kind of fern. Hairs from a fox's tail. We thought she was sending us on an excursion, you see. That she was giving us our independence, letting us roam all over the place like that. Until one afternoon my brother Buck tripped on a root and broke his tooth. Me and Tad had to carry him back, bawling."

Grandpa Howe mimics lugging his youngest brother down the path. Grandma Tess laughs again, but a funny feeling has started swimming around in my head, and I can't join her this time.

"Loud as Buck was screaming," Grandpa Howe goes on, "we could hear Pop cussing over those boards and shingles long before we reached the house. There were nails and scraps everywhere. Place was a mess. He'd been doing that every day, Mother making him clean up before we got home. Sometimes, just barely."

"Oh, I can just imagine your poor mother," Grandma Tess says.

I've seen photos of Great-Grandma Rachel, even of her at the End of the Road with Grandpa Howe and his brothers when they were young. But right now all I see is Grandpa Howe and me, biking together on our own to the Custard Cup a few days before we left on this trip. We had just finished printing out the itinerary and weren't able to wait for Grandma Tess to get back from her yoga class to celebrate. While we rode, savoring the sunshine and our sense of satisfaction, Grandpa Howe smiled at me and said, "It's a good thing, this honeymoon, isn't it?"

I told him it was going to be fantastic. And I didn't think very much about it when he'd said next, "I think the timing is just right for you."

Now, after the story of Grandpa Howe's mother sending him away on "adventures" so that he and his brothers wouldn't know how badly the new porch was going, his talk about timing echoes in my head. All my parents could focus on in the days before I left was what an adventure this was going to be. They were so eager to see what I'd come back with and said they couldn't imagine a better way for me to get a little more independence. Grandpa Howe went on and on about what a great time we were going to have, and even Grandma Tess told me one afternoon, when I was over there during one of Mom's headaches, that she understood how I might want to get away and have some fun.

I know for certain now that just like when Grandpa Howe's dad was building the porch, my parents need me out of the house. All that stuff about adventure and fun was just to get me out the door. Really Mom and Dad sent me away—and Grandpa Howe and Grandma Tess agreed to take me—so I won't have to see how sick Mom is. How everything is falling apart.

Chapter Twelve

Cassie

I don't think of bakers as a big celebrities, but the energy in the demo kitchen once we get to Visalia feels more like a concert than a cooking class. I know Howie and Lana are excited, but I'm surprised how into it Nono is. My whole life, Nono's cooking abilities covered mainly spaghetti or lentil soup. The only time she wears an apron is for her art. Now, while we're waiting for Brick Hasselback to appear, she's singing, "If I knew you were coming, I'd've baked you a *cup*cake!" and bouncing like a little kid.

I decide to bounce along, only so Nono's enthusiasm will wash over me, too. After that whole bit with Lana this morning, plus Cheyenne Taylor bugging me about tennis, and those pictures Izzy Gathing sent me in the car of her horseback-riding session with Kendra Mack, I need some of my Nono right now. Not to mention something that will help block Fiona from my mind. I was thinking of her way too much at Hearst Castle. Her, and Cory Baxter.

"It's starting." Nono motions to the screens overhead. They're flashing scenes from the cupcake show—towers of them toppling over, others held together in incredible sculptures. People at the other workstations are clapping and cheering, many of them holding copies of Brick Hasselback's new cookbook. I guess this guy is a big deal.

A voice comes out through the speakers: "Here he is, ladies and gentlemen, award-winning confectioner and host of *Cupstructions*—Brick Hasselback!"

The room goes even crazier, and Howie whistles. Beside me Nono lets out a long "Wooot." Lana grins up at both of them like she won a million dollars. When Brick Hasselback bounds out onto the stage, shouting hello to everyone in his green-and-white-striped baker's apron, I can see what the fuss is about. He is drop-dead gorgeous. And Australian.

Lana leans in and says something close to my ear, but I can't hear her over the noise. I nod anyway and briefly wish phones were allowed in the cooking studio. But I already texted Kendra Mack twice about good-looking boys, and neither of them was the one I really want to be talking about.

"All right, everybody, we're going to have a fun afternoon here," Brick Hasselback says, "but the key is going to be working together."

Together. Right.

He goes on to describe the ingredients at our station and what we'll be doing first. I try to focus. We divide up the tasks—Nono and Howie measuring out dry ingredients, Lana and I mixing the butter and eggs. As we work, thoughts of Fiona still keep mixing in my mind, even though I don't want them to. Talking to Lana about my "boyfriend" is nice, and it's flattering that Kendra Mack is so curious about my crush, but Fiona's the only person who truly knows and understands everything about Cory Baxter. She was with me, after all, on that day I saw him waiting in line to get milk shakes and laughing with his friends. She's the one I told about the sudden flutter in my heart I hadn't ever felt before, when I realized that not only did I think Cory was cute, but I also wanted to *know* him.

Fiona already had a crush on Tyrick Nevin in her English class, so she knew exactly what I meant. She'd only been referring to Tyrick by his code name, Pencil, for a week or so, but it meant we could discuss him without anyone else knowing. She dubbed Cory "Lagoon," for his blue eyes.

Pencil was in several of Fiona's classes, but I hardly saw

Cory at school. So Fiona and I roamed the halls and court-yards, trying to find out where he hung out, where his locker was, and who his friends were. We were nervous, since Cory was an eighth grader, but pretending we belonged in their hall was fun and helped us imagine ourselves there next year. When we figured out Cory's schedule, Fiona planned the best shortcuts between my classes so that I could pass him in the hall. She watched *Doctor Who* and *Sherlock* episodes with me after we overheard him talking about them, and I listened as she read poems out loud that she thought Pencil might like. We agreed it was a good idea for us to have something to talk about with our crushes.

Now I know for real how Fiona felt about all that, thanks to the Diary Incident.

"All right now," Brick Hasselback says, holding up an ice cream scoop. "This little guy is your best friend when it comes to doling out the batter."

Best friend, ha. Best friend who thinks you're shallow but won't tell you to your face. Who writes it in her diary for everyone else to find. My cheeks burn, thinking of that day again, even as the four of us take turns spooning cake batter into cupcake tins.

Fiona and I were on the way to science, talking about something intense, when we realized she'd forgotten her backpack in the cafeteria. I went with her to find it, even though it would make me late, too. We didn't say anything, but I know we were both envisioning her cute red bag covered in chili or worse.

In the lunchroom, we breathed a sigh of relief. Someone had kicked Fiona's bag under another chair not far from our table. She was worried something was stolen, but as she dug through the pockets, it seemed her wallet, books, phone, and keys were all intact.

"My diary," she said after a minute. "I think it's gone."

My immediate reaction was a confusing burst of irritation. I knew she didn't want to leave her diary at home where her mom or her sister might get to it, but still. How did she think this wouldn't happen?

When she turned to me with that look on her face, though, all I could feel was sad for her, and scared. After we got to science class and explained, Mrs. Tasker let Fiona go back to the cafeteria for a more extensive search, but she wasn't gone long, and when she came back, I could tell she was trying to look brave. I didn't think there could be anything more embarrassing than some random person reading through all your private thoughts and dreams, and I felt awful for her.

Turned out, though, there was something worse— Kendra Mack reading them. Out loud. On the bus.

"So while those are doing their baking," our handsome

instructor says, flashing a TV smile, "it's time to get on to the best part—the icing."

The women at the station beside us screech in a way I didn't think people their age could. Nono raises her eyebrows to Howie, and Lana reaches for more butter.

"This is the best part," she tells me. "Here. You pour in the sugar."

She hands me a giant measuring cup filled with confectioner's sugar. As I pour it in the bowl, too fast, a cloud of it rises up into my face. I blink hard to keep back the tears, just like that day on the bus.

I'd been riding the same bus as Kendra Mack since sixth grade, when she climbed up the steps with her sleek hair and her super-stylish outfit and strode all the way down the aisle to the backseat, where the eighth graders sat, just like she belonged there. She was so confident, no one questioned it. Not even the eighth graders. Kendra Mack and her sidekick neighbor Gates Morrill have held court back there every day since. Until we became friends, she didn't pay attention to me and I didn't pay attention to her, except for checking out her outfit or eavesdropping on a conversation or two.

After school on the Diary Incident day, Kendra Mack and Gates Morrill were already back there, hunched together over something I couldn't see. Kendra Mack could barely keep her giggles inside the cup of her fingers. Gates Morrill kept trying to grab whatever they were looking at, but she'd only shove him in the chest with her elbow, hard. As seats started filling up, every now and again I'd hear one of them say, "Let me see," or "Read something." I figured they were talking about something that didn't concern me and ignored them as best I could.

When I heard the word *Pencil*, though, my whole body tingled.

"Who the heck is *Pencil*?" Gates Morrill said for the benefit of everyone.

"Some dork, duh," Kendra Mack answered. "Ha, listen to this."

Everything inside me was groaning *no*. *No* that Kendra Mack had my best friend's journal. *No* that she was reading it out loud for everyone on the bus, and *no* because there wasn't anything I could do to stop it.

"'I know I'm far too young to experience Real Love like my parents, but Pencil isn't smelly and goofy like half the boys in our school.'" Kendra Mack paused and guffawed, "Like you, Gates Morrill!"

"As if," he said, and everyone laughed like it was a good comeback.

"'Instead he seems to have real interests, and a real soul. A soul that maybe wants to understand mine.'"

Fiona sounded so dumb that even I was wincing. I clenched my teeth and my eyes together at the same time, wanting to bite off the sound of Kendra Mack's voice forever. It was torture waiting for their stop. At least when they got off they'd only have each other to share Fee's diary with.

"Ooh, snap, you're in here!" Gates shouted, and Kendra Mack squealed.

Our bus driver told everybody to keep it down, but all I wanted was more noise to drown all this out.

Gates Morrill took on a fake-girl voice and read, "'I really don't understand why Cassie admires Kendra so much. She's not that special. We both know those kids have money and looks and nothing else. Most of the time not even looks. But maybe Cassie doesn't care any longer about being something more. Even with Lagoon she's more worried lately about does he think she's pretty, or that the "wrong" people will find out she likes him. Honestly, I worry she's getting a little bit shallow.'"

I was so stunned, I hardly heard whatever they said next.

Now I shudder, remembering, glad for the block of chocolate Nono's handing me. Howie comes over, trying to show me the right way, but I take the grater and tell him I know how to do it. The friction of pressing down feels good. I imagine I'm pressing down on Fiona's face.

"What's with these super-dumb nicknames?" Gates Morrill had said, back in his regular voice. "Pencil? Lagoon? At least come up with something cool, like Shark Tank or Ninja Thunder."

"She's trying to be deep, dummy," Kendra Mack said back. "But really she's lame." Practically the entire bus was snickering.

I hated that they were calling Fiona lame, and that I wasn't doing anything about it. I hated that Kendra Mack and everyone who was listening now knew about Cory, even though I was grateful Fiona hadn't called him by his real name. If Kendra Mack kept reading on, though, and Fiona forgot the code word, it would be all over school in less than a minute.

But worse than all that was hearing what Fiona said about *me* in there. That I was *shallow*. I certainly wanted to be more than pretty. Why else would I have been in so many clubs, and worked so hard to keep my GPA higher than even Tom's? I wasn't sure it was wrong to want Cory to think I looked nice. Fiona could talk about *soul* all she wanted, but she'd started wearing green a lot more once she found out it was Pencil's favorite color. And it's not like clothes aren't important to her, too. Was it so wrong to pay attention to what Kendra Mack likes, if only to stay on trend?

Fiona shouldn't have left her backpack in the lunchroom

in the first place. She should have been more responsible. Thanks to her, now Kendra Mack and everyone else had access to *both* our secrets. Thanks to her, everyone knew I had a crush.

"Oh, that looks like plenty," Howie says, reaching for the heaping pile of chocolate I've grated. I feel embarrassed, a little, until Nono reaches over and grabs a pinch to pop in her mouth.

"Extra never hurt." She winks.

"This is gonna be sooo good," Lana says, watching Howie slowly mix the shaved chocolate into our fluffy icing. I move out of the way in a daze as Nono opens the oven to take out our admittedly delicious-smelling cupcakes. Brick Hasselback starts guiding us on to mixing the raspberry jelly for the middles, while the cupcakes are cooling. One of his assistants comes to whisk our cutting board away in the transition, but before she does I press my finger into the remaining shreds of chocolate, needing to taste something sweet.

I know I should've tried to stop Kendra Mack. With the bus moving, though, I couldn't stand up and go back there. And getting the diary away from Gates Morrill would've been impossible. Being confused about how I felt was what really kept me in my seat, though. There were so many layers of mad and sad and sick and awful heaping up inside me, and I thought the bus ride would never end.

Finally, it was Kendra Mack and Gates Morrill's stop. They said good-bye to their friends and ambled up the aisle, still laughing. Right as Kendra Mack passed by my seat, she looked straight down at me.

"Oh," she said, surprised and then amused. "We didn't see you."

I wanted to say that noticing other people and their feelings didn't seem to be one of her specialties, no. Or anything that would make her feel sheepish.

"Fiona thinks those things," I said instead, a coward. "But I don't. I didn't even know she did until right now."

Kendra Mack snorted and hoisted her expensive purse farther up on her shoulder.

"Yeah, well, if you ask me, it's pretty chicken to hide your true thoughts in a little diary like that. Not to mention false. And immature. You should be outraged, actually."

"I—"

"Miss Mack, other children need to get home too," our bus driver called.

"I'm coming." But Kendra Mack turned back to me first. "Maybe you're actually growing up and she's holding you back, right?"

I couldn't say anything. That Kendra Mack was being slightly nice to me—that she even knew who I was—was enough of a shock. The rest of it was even harder to attach thoughts to.

That night I avoided Fiona's texts and attempts to chat, and the next day I still didn't know how to feel. I was mad at Fiona for what she'd said about me and couldn't help wondering what other bad things she had written. What else did Kendra Mack know, instead of me? Still, I knew I'd wronged Fiona by not standing up for her. Fiona was the kind of friend who patiently listened until you'd gotten everything out, even the things you hadn't known you'd felt until you started saying them, so I knew even though I was mad—and she might be too—talking it through was the best thing to do.

By lunch I was brave enough to face her. I was heading for the table where we usually sat, relieved to see her waiting for me, when Kendra Mack hollered, "Hey, Cassie Parker, where you headed?" like I'd been sitting with her group all year long. I paused for just a step before turning my back on the table, and my best friend.

"And now for our assembly," Brick Hasselback says, wielding a serrated knife. Up on the screen, there's an overhead view of his hands as he slices a cupcake in half. He smears one side with raspberry jelly. He places the other half gently over it and uses a mini ice cream scoop to mound the chocolate-flaked icing on top.

"And there you have it," he says as the screens above fill with a close-up of the finished cupcake. "Of course, don't be afraid if it makes a bit of a mess." He holds up a jelly-coated finger and smiles that smile again. More ladies around us squeal and titter.

I help Lana cut the cupcakes in half while Nono's on jelly duty and Howie scoops the icing. We get a rhythm going, the four of us, though it is indeed a bit of a mess.

Not as big a mess as me and Fiona. We haven't talked since. She never even tried to call. It's as though when I walked away from our table, I walked right off Fiona's planet. I only found out she'd gotten her journal back when Izzy Gathing said something about it a couple of days later at lunch. I guess I was glad, but mostly there was that hot, confusing ball of shame and anger inside me that I didn't know what to do with. So I buried it down and spent the rest of the school year trying to keep up with Kendra Mack and the rest of my new friends.

I've still kept my crush on Cory Baxter, of course, but after listening to Cheyenne Taylor and Neftali Manji talk incessantly about the boys they like—and hearing how Kendra Mack and Izzy Gathing shoot them down—I'm still unsure about revealing who Lagoon really is. Thanks to stupid Fiona, though, Kendra Mack won't let up with the Loverboy stuff, and it's getting a lot harder to hide the truth from her. Being away from everyone this week only makes it worse. When I'm home, I can at least let their conversations take over. I only have to laugh at the right time, be in the right place, or say the right thing in response to someone else. Away from them all it's more of a challenge.

"Now, these aren't the kind of cupcakes you can build an Eiffel Tower with," Brick Hasselback says, holding one up, "but it's how I got my start, and I wanted to share it with all of you. So dig in and enjoy your hard work, and I'll get to signing in a moment." He grins again before taking a big bite.

The lights go up, and Nono wipes her hands on her apron to give us all high fives. Howie offers the first cupcakes to me and Lana, and she raises hers, smiling.

"Let's have a toast," she says.

I lift mine along with Nono and Howie, trying not to get my fingers in the sticky jelly leaking from the sides.

"To . . . ," Lana starts, but a strange expression crosses her face, like she doesn't know what to say. She looks up at Howie.

"To accomplishing something delicious together," he says.

We clink our cupcakes and take bites. Even though thinking about Fiona fills me with nothing but bitterness, I have to admit they are delicious.

97

Chapter Thirteen

Lana

Having so much fun at the baking class with Cassie, Grandma Tess, and Grandpa Howe helps my worry about Mom take the back burner for a while. The cupcakes were amazing, Brick Hasselback was so charming, and Grandma Tess's excitement was even bigger than mine and Grandpa Howe's put together. Even Cassie got into it, making sure we had plenty of chocolate flake in that icing, which is why I'm a little surprised she's so quiet in the car. She still hasn't uttered a word since we've checked into the Visalia hotel and gone up to our room to change for dinner.

"It would've been fun if we'd been able to build a crazy cupcake tower," I say, wondering if that's what she's disappointed about, since Brick Hasselback is so famous for it. Maybe plain cupcakes weren't quite cool enough.

"Mmm." She nods faintly. "You mind if I wash up?"

"Go ahead."

I have no idea what's bothering her, but it's strangely still in the room when she closes the bathroom door. I try to turn my attention to getting ready for dinner, reminding myself that tonight's restaurant is going to be even better than cupcakes. Broadway! has themed dining wings, each decorated around a different Broadway musical. The servers dress up in costumes and sing songs from your show, and even the menu matches. Cassie and I really haven't talked a lot about movies or music or anything, so I don't know exactly how into musicals she is, but I absolutely love them. Teaching Grandma Tess all my favorite songs has been so fun, I'm hoping it'll be the same with Cassie.

"Grandma Tess and I want to get seated in *Wicked*," I try again with Cassie when she comes back out.

She doesn't look at me but at her shoes instead, like she's trying to decide if she wants to change them. "Is that right?" she says. I can't help but notice the tense sound in her voice.

The way she's acting makes me think about our fight before, and how she was mad without me knowing it. "Cassie, did I do anything wrong?"

"I don't know what you mean."

I'm not sure what I mean, either. "You just seem sort of quiet, and I was wondering if you needed to tell me anything."

"I don't want to talk about it." She tucks her afternoon outfit into her dirty clothes bag. "It's almost time to go, anyway."

I'm a little relieved, because whatever's upsetting her, it doesn't seem like it's me this time. But I also understand about not wanting to talk about things better than she thinks I might. In my experience, feeling that way is more about thinking you don't have anyone around to really listen, and I don't want Cassie to believe that about me.

"I just mean that if there's something that's bothering you, you can talk to me about it and I won't say anything to anyone else. You don't know this about me yet, but I'm very good at keeping secrets. In fact, Rule Number Six is one that pretty much goes without saying, and that is that Anything You Tell Me Is a Secret, Unless You Say Otherwise."

"What do you know about secrets?" she mutters, so quiet I almost don't hear her.

Suddenly the room is charged with an energy that makes my scalp and eyes prickle. I know a lot about secrets, actually. First there's the secret my parents and grandparents seem to be keeping about exactly how sick my mom is, but there's also the one I've been keeping from them: how scared and sad I am about it all. Maybe, I think, Cassie already knows about my mom, if Grandma Tess told her parents. Maybe she's been waiting for me to bring it up this whole time.

"I know better than you think I do," I tell her.

Our eyes meet, and for a second, the secrets rise up from my stomach and hover at the back of my mouth, wanting to come out. I've been too worried it'll make bad things come true if I say my suspicions about Mom dying out loud, even to Grandpa Howe, but with Cassie here, and both of us needing a good listener, I realize I might spill everything right now. Maybe she would too.

My lips part, and I take in a breath.

A knock at the door makes us both jump.

"You girls all set?" Grandma Tess calls.

I glance back at Cassie, wanting to hang on to whatever that just was, but the moment's broken, and she's already heading out.

Grandma Tess is still buzzing with the sugar and the excitement from this afternoon. In the car she tells Cassie a story I adore: her first date with Grandpa Howe, when they were supposed to go out for lunch, but Grandma Tess got so into her painting she lost track of time and stood him up. So he ended up bringing a picnic to her house.

"I'd never had homemade macarons before," Grandma Tess says, "so I had no idea what he'd gone through to make them, not to mention the rest of the spread. I've gained a much better appreciation for it now, though."

"Appreciation for the process or the end result?" Grandpa Howe chuckles.

Grandma Tess glances at him with admiration. "Both equally, I think. Though there was a lot I wasn't noticing that day, including the swipe of Prussian Blue paint I had across my cheek." I can see her embarrassed smile in the rearview. "Didn't notice it was there until Howie'd been gone for an hour."

"You look beautiful in blue," Grandpa Howe says. "Beautiful in anything, really. I love that memory— you, talking so excitedly, with that splash of color there. Lovely."

Grandma Tess takes his hand, and the warm, happy feeling I always get when they're like this washes over me, though it also makes me miss my parents. I decide I need to talk to them before dinner. I want to check on them both, for one, but also I don't like keeping the truth about my mother from Cassie. The problem is, I don't actually know what the truth really is, so it's time to ask. Finding out feels scary, but then I won't have to lie to Cassie—or anybody else.

Before I can think myself out of it, I ask if it's okay if I call them when we get to the restaurant, explaining that waiting until after dinner might be too late.

Grandma Tess answers without hesitating. "Of course you can, Lana. You don't need to ask."

So, when we get to Broadway!, though I'm dying to get inside, I tell them to go on in without me.

"Do you want me to wait out here with you?" Grandpa Howe offers.

Suddenly both Grandma Tess and Grandpa Howe are putting too much attention on this phone call. For a second I think about saying forget it, and that I'll text Dad later, but now Cassie's watching me too. I don't want to act so weird that she starts asking me questions I don't have the answers to.

"I'm fine." I wave them into the restaurant, like this is no big deal and will only take a second. Grandma Tess opens the door for Cassie, and strains of "I Could Have Danced All Night" from *My Fair Lady* come streaming out. Grandpa Howe takes another glance back at me. His concerned expression, mixed with the sound of the music, makes me want to run into the escape of that restaurant so bad that I press the speed dial for Dad, quick before I chicken out.

He answers after not even two rings. "Lanalee! How's the adventuring?"

The sound of his voice makes my nose tingle with missing him. So that I don't cry right off the bat, I tell him about cupcake making and the restaurant we're at now.

"Grandpa's not feeding you flayed octopus tentacles and birds' nests lined with kale-pomegranate crunch yet, is he?"

I smile. "Mostly it's been a lot of ice cream."

"Good girl."

"How's Mom today?" I ask, to keep from beating around the bush.

He sighs. "Ah, not the best day, I'm afraid. I made her take off early and head home. I almost came with her, it's so abnormally hot out, but there were things to finish up. She's in the bath now, though, and you know how that improves things. How are you and Cassie getting along?"

I'm so surprised that Mom left work early—something she only does if I'm sick, and even then she brings work home—it takes me a minute to process his question. "Um. We're having fun together." Distracting images of Mom suffering a headache in the heat make it hard to answer. "Sometimes she can get quiet. Like there's something wrong but she won't say."

"Well, sometimes people need their space," Dad says. "A chance to sort out everything before they can share it with anyone else, you know? Maybe that's what's happening with Cassie right now. I'm sure she'll talk to you when she's ready."

My panic revs even higher. I know without a doubt that Dad's sending me a coded message about Mom. Sometimes people need space. As in, sometimes people need a week with their daughter away so that they can figure out how to break the most terrible news to her, ever.

They're still not going to tell me yet. Not even if it's getting worse.

"It looks like you're managing to have an okay time, anyway," Dad goes on. "Your pictures are gorgeous. Tell Grandpa Howe he's going to have to step it up a notch for the next father-son fishing trip, now that I see what he's treating you to."

I let out a little laugh, but my chest feels like someone is stepping on it. As Dad winds down the conversation, saying he knows I must be dying to get into that restaurant, I have to blow out a big, slow breath so the fear and homesickness won't take over. That he isn't even offering to hand the phone to Mom in the tub means it's really bad. Before I know it, we're swapping "I love yous," I'm promising to send photos of the restaurant, and then he's gone.

As I climb up the front steps and haul open the heavy door on my own, I'm not sure any amount of singing and dancing can turn things around for me tonight.

Chapter Fourteen

Cassie

The next morning at breakfast, Nono announces we're going to an art festival in the park, before heading out to the next town. This is no surprise, unlike last night when she and Lana kept breaking into all these different show tunes I'd never heard before, like this is some special thing they do together now. Lana seemed weird after her phone call, but Nono had asked the hostess if we could sit in the *Wicked* section, and before long Lana had perked up. The cauldron of chocolate fondue Howie ordered before dinner probably didn't hurt.

But looking at art is my thing with Nono. She has such a great sense of color and style, and I always learn things—or at least, get new things—from her. I'm glad that for my outfit of the day I had already pulled on the batik T-shirt Nono made for me at Christmas. When Lana and I go back up for our suitcases, I switch into the silver beaded earrings Nono and I picked together in San Francisco last year.

"Oh, I love those, Cassie," Nono says when Lana and I are back down with our stuff in the lobby.

I smile at her. "I do too still."

She tucks her arm around me. When Howie finishes checking us out of the hotel, Nono's arm stays put. We head out into the sunshine that way together, just me and her—no silly songs needed. Still, there's a lot that Lana seems to know about Nono and I don't, so I ask about her latest project.

"Silk-screening, I think," she tells me. "It's complicated, and takes a lot of equipment, but you can do some amazing things with it. At least from what I've seen."

"Here we go," I tease her. Nono's studio is already crowded with a pottery wheel, an antique photo enlarger, enough beads and shells to run her own bead store, plus her paints, finished and half-finished canvases, and three or four easels. All because she thinks she can do amazing things with them. And usually does.

"You know everything I learn from new projects informs the others." She's pretending to sound hurt.

"I like it," I assure her. "You're like a butterfly, going from flower to flower."

She flaps her fingers like little wings and makes a pleased face. "Well, let's see what this little garden has to offer us, shall we?"

It doesn't take very long at the festival to see that Nono's butterflying art is way better than a lot of the stuff here. Still, Nono is sweet to everyone, asking them about their processes and finding a way to pay each of them a genuine compliment, even a small one.

"Grandma Tess is always so friendly," Lana whispers as we gawk around a stall full of quilts made with tacky iridescent fabrics.

"It's an art form," I insist, not sure she means it as a nice thing. "You can learn a lot of people skills by watching Nono."

Lana looks apologetic. "Oh, I know that. I think it's wonderful. I just mean"—she lifts her hands to the magenta-and-orange sparkly quilt hanging in front of us—"the color here. And what you did with the spirals. It's so . . . vibrant." Her voice is full of false awe, and she smiles sideways at me.

"Well, it's nothing compared to these," I tell her, moving to the next stall over. It's filled with plant hangers woven out of what look like recycled grocery store bags. "I had to go shopping for months."

Lana giggles. "I see. They must've taken so much work."

I hold out my hands to her. "You wouldn't believe the blisters."

Nono and Howie join us as we're laughing.

"See anything you like?" Howie asks, gazing at the plants above us.

"Oh yes," Lana says. "I was just telling Cassie I want one of these planters for Christmas."

Howie's eyebrows go up in surprise. "Well, it'd certainly be interesting."

Of course he doesn't get it.

"I don't know, Lana," Nono says, strolling across to the next stall. She picks up a chip bowl painted with pink flamingos inside. There's a smaller bowl to put the dip in, one that's the actual shape of a flamingo. It hooks onto the bigger bowl by its beak. "I was thinking of getting you this."

"Oh, perfect," I say, happy Nono's playing too. "And I think I've found just the thing for your kitchen." I gesture to another stall down from us, full of framed embroidery that says things like WORLD'S BEST GRANDMA, and IF YOU CAN'T SAY SOMETHING NICE, COME STAND NEXT TO ME.

"Fabulous," Nono says. "I think I want four."

We go on like that from stall to stall, secretly picking out the most ridiculous items to "give" each other for Christmas or our birthdays. Not everything is terrible, though. Howie buys a set of beautiful, hand-carved wooden salad servers, and Lana points out a wind chime made from antique spoons and forks that we all like. There's an etching Nono and I agree would look nice in my dad's office, and when she decides to go ahead and buy it, I stay with her while she talks to the artist about shipping it to Monterey. Howie and Lana take off to watch the papier-mâché sculpting demonstration together, so before we join them, Nono and I circle back to the best jewelry stall. We stack our wrists with bangles and hold up earrings next to each other's ears, trying to decide which matching set we should get.

"Lana should have a pair too," Nono says, leaning closer to one of the earring stands. "Which do you think she'd like best?"

Right. Lana, too.

"Is she much of a jewelry type, though?" The way Lana keeps her things, I imagine she'd just lose them immediately. And besides, I don't want her and Nono to match in this way. They've already got all kinds of other moments.

"Well, not the same way we are," Nono agrees. "But I think she'd like to be. It would be fun to help her, right?"

Lana could definitely use some help when it comes to accessorizing. Or dressing. And that hair of hers. I'm not totally keen on the idea, but having a special project, just me and Nono—even if it is Lana—might be the kind of fun I always miss between our visits. So after some debate about length and glitteriness, we decide on a pair of small hoops made of sparkly beads. They're less dramatic than the ones Nono and I get for ourselves, but they're still pretty. Lana's look of surprise and delight when we give them to her, and the proud way Nono says that I picked them out, make me feel happy in a way only being with Nono can.

Even the drive between Visalia and our next stop is pleasant. Howie works a crossword puzzle in the front seat, asking Nono the clues he can't get, and Lana and I each read our own things. After a while Lana asks Nono to play the sound track from *Once* so that I can learn a song we overheard at the restaurant last night that the two of them loved so much. The music is beautiful, even if it's sad. Lana and Nono are singing, and I'm caught up in the rise of their voices melding together with the stereo when my phone *bing*s in my purse.

"Oh, Cassie, wait until the song's over at least," Nono says, turning down the volume as I reach for it.

"It'll just take a second," I tell her. I haven't texted with Kendra Mack at all today.

What's up? is all she says.

Driving to the next town now, I type quick.

What'd you do this morning? she fires back.

Art festival.

Get anything good?

Cool earrings. I wince after I hit send, knowing she'll probably want pictures.

I wanna see, she says, of course.

Can't right now, I hurry. The song has played through and Nono's paused the sound track, waiting for me to finish before we listen to the next one.

Tell me something good then. No one's around & it's boring.

My gma's husband always orders dessert first, I try. **Every meal.**

Tell me something GOOD, I said. Something I actually want to know.

"You are aware, Cassie," Nono warns, "that we're waiting on you to finish your conversation, right? This has been such a nice day so far."

"Okay, just one more minute," I say, feeling trapped. I do want to keep having fun with Nono, but this is also the first time Kendra Mack has turned to me alone for entertainment, and I need to hold her attention a little longer.

You have to promise not to tell anyone else, I stall. Kendra Mack always loves a good secret. I just have to think of one.

Ooh, that's more like it. What's up?

This is just btwn you & me.

Of course. What is it?

But nothing is coming to mind. Nothing good enough. **You have to swear.**

Cross my heart!

"Cassie, please," Nono says, losing her patience. "You really will lose phone privileges if it keeps interrupting us this way."

"I'm sorry." Ugh. I can't think of anything juicy for Kendra Mack with Nono rushing me. The only real secret I have is one I've been trying to keep from her for months.

But it's all I've got. I only pause a moment before I send: **Cory Baxter.**

This time it takes her a few beats to respond: **Really?**

You're my bestie so I thought u shld know. But listen, I have to go. Promise this is just btwn us, right?

"Cassie, really," Nono says, hitting the steering wheel with her palm. "This is getting beyond rude."

"I know, I'm sorry," I say, my heart in my chest. Not

because Nono's getting mad, but because I can't quite believe I just told Kendra Mack about Cory Baxter. I need to hear her say she won't tell anyone else before I put my phone away. I need her to say it's okay. "Just one last thing, I swear. It's Tom, and he's—" I lie, right as another text comes in.

I wouldn't tell anyone a thing like that.

I let go of the breath I was holding. You're the best! TTYL, ok?

Her message, Oh definitely, blinks across my screen. I lean forward, relieved, and apologize to Nono again, asking that we crank the music back up, nice and loud.

I don't even know what town our new hotel is in, but it doesn't matter because at least there's a good pool. Apparently the main reason we drove here is for the restaurant we're going to tonight—a place Howie found that serves a different kind of pie for each state in America. I still think the man is a little too obsessed with dessert to be healthy, but it has made mealtimes pretty delicious.

When Lana and I finish changing into our swimsuits and head to the rooftop deck, I decide to leave my phone behind. Part because of Nono's warning in the car, part because it needs to be charged anyway, and part because I need a break. I trust Kendra Mack—I do—but I also know how carried away she can get. How things sometimes slip out. Like the time she accidentally blurted to Neftali Manji what Cheyenne Taylor said about her being a fashion copy-cat, after she saw Neftali's new jeans. It's just a thing that happens sometimes. Kendra Mack's always apologetic, and everyone understands. I just don't want to be around my phone if she accidentally blurts my secret crush to some-one like Izzy Gathing.

Lana brings hers down, though, which is a little strange. I can't quite picture Lana having the urgent need to text Tamika, who apparently is off at camp anyway. Certainly she won't be hearing from that Henry guy.

I don't think about any of it too much, because in gen-eral it's a perfect afternoon. We swim and play around in the pool awhile, then all four stretch out in the sun. There are signs everywhere that say NO DIVING, because this pool isn't really that deep, and they prompt Howie to tell a story about the swimming hole near the End of the Road, and how he and his brothers used to dare each other to try and find the bottom.

"No one has yet," he says, voice full of fake mystery.

Lana squints at him in the sun. "Them's fighting words, Grandpa Howe."

"I'll say," Nono adds.

"Well, one day I'll toss you both in headfirst—see if

you can fare better than the Howe brothers. You'd be hard-pressed to try harder than Tad did. I'd pay to see it."

"Would you pay in pie?" I tease him, thinking of later tonight.

"You know what, Cassie? I just might."

I stand up, reaching for Lana's hand. "Come on, then," I tell her. "We better get some practice." And with that we both jump in, feet first, swimming to sit on the bottom and see who can hold her breath the longest.

Chapter Fifteen

Lana

Except for when Cassie was going back and forth with Kendra Mack on her phone and Grandma Tess started getting irritated, I'd say that yesterday definitely helped me feel somewhat better. Mom and I texted several times during the papier-mâché demonstration Grandpa Howe and I were watching, and she loved all the pictures I sent. She was back at work too, which at least was an improvement from the day before. Swimming around in the water and stretching out in the sunshine that afternoon also helped relax my muscles. When we got to Pie Country that night, Cassie was so won over by the different kinds of pie there (orange meringue for Florida, pineapple coconut cream for Hawaii, cheese and onion pie for Wisconsin) that in honor of Grandpa Howe's find, she proclaimed Rule Number Seven to be Dessert First, which made me feel good.

After breakfast, when we're getting our things together to head out to Bakersfield, though, Cassie checks her phone and groans, "Oh no."

Suddenly my whole body's pulsing with panic again. It would be horrible if Cassie got bad news on this trip, too. "What is it?"

She holds up her hand, firm, reminding me of Rule Number Two: Don't Talk to Me While I Have My Phone. I start gathering my things from the desk, but the back of my neck is prickling, waiting for her to finish scrolling through whatever it is she's looking at.

"Cassie, is everything okay?" I can't help asking. If something happened to her brother, or her parents—

"Kendra Mack was at Izzy Gathing's house last night," is all she says.

My shoulders relax, but I'm still confused. Done with my packing, I plop into the one armchair in our room and just wait. Cassie starts typing, a deep frown on her face. Immediately an answering *bing* chimes in.

"Grandma Tess and Grandpa Howe are waiting downstairs," I remind her.

"I know," she growls. "But I've got to take care of this."

"Did something happen?"

She doesn't look away from her phone. "Her brother's in the same grade as Cory Baxter."

"Kendra Mack has a brother too?"

"Not Kendra Mack," she snaps. "Izzy Gathing."

This still doesn't make any sense, but I don't say anything else because Cassie's typing again. This time, when the answer comes back in, she starts blushing and breaks into an enormous grin.

"Oh. My. Gosh." She holds her phone to her chest and finally looks at me. "Kendra Mack is the best friend in the world."

I'm not sure I quite agree with that, but I try not to show it.

"She was over at Izzy Gathing's last night," she goes on, "and got the idea to look up Cory Baxter. That's why I was upset at first, because I don't want Izzy Gathing knowing all my business, but apparently it was her idea to get in touch with him for me. And he asked for my number!"

I feel my eyebrows scrunch down before I can stop them. "But doesn't he have your number already?"

Cassie looks down at her phone like she's never seen it before. "Oh. Well, no. Because, you know, we see each other at school."

"But you said you don't have classes with him, so isn't

after school your best time to talk?" I'm not trying to make Cassie feel bad—it's just that I don't quite understand how all of this works.

She shakes her head and sighs. "Like I said, my parents are strict. And anyway, this means he wants to take it to the next level."

Something still feels off, but I can't argue with the delighted expression on Cassie's face. Until yet another message comes in, and she frowns again.

"Shut up, Izzy Gathing," she mutters. When she sees me watching, she explains, "Just Izzy Gathing being snide."

"That's not very nice."

"Izzy Gathing isn't very nice. It's, like, her job to be mean. The more you can put up with, the better. It's like a test."

"Annoying test if you ask me," I grumble under my breath, ready for this to be over and for us to get going.

She's heard me, though. "Maybe you should mind your own business."

That she's turning on me when it's her friends who are difficult makes me lose my patience. "Maybe I would, if you'd stop dragging me into it. All you talk about is what's going on with Kendra Mack and Cheyenne What's-Her-Head. It's all you seem to care about. Maybe Grandma Tess *should* take your phone."

"Fine." Cassie stands up and yanks her giant suitcase to the door. "If you're not interested in what people with *real* lives actually do, instead of playing stupid shopping games and taking fake glamour shots, I won't bother you with it anymore."

It's so mean, I'm shocked. Cassie genuinely seemed to be having fun with all that stuff. I don't know what else to say except, "Well, don't, then."

"Good."

She huffs out of the room, dragging her bags, and I have no choice but to follow.

To make things worse, it's a longer drive today to Bakersfield, and no matter how many routes we looked at, Grandpa Howe and I couldn't find any way to get there that involved many interesting road stops.

"We haven't had trouble entertaining each other so far," Grandma Tess says happily, connecting her iPod to the stereo.

I'm not really up for singing right now, especially since it's something else I love to do that Cassie probably thinks is stupid, but I lean forward in my seat and wrap my arms around Grandpa Howe's headrest and hum a little, anyway. It's better than pouting out the window, like Cassie is doing.

After an hour, I'm hollering out "I'm in Love with a Big Blue Frog" and "Break on Through," not caring what Cassie thinks anymore, which is just as well because her mood only seems to have gotten blacker. This playlist of Grandma Tess's has a bunch of old stuff on it, but it's also pretty fun. If Cassie can't enjoy it, that's her loss. When a disco song starts, Grandma Tess lets out a wild laugh and hits the brake. Grandpa Howe peers through his spectacles at the dashboard and asks is everything okay.

"Oh, everything's fine!" Grandma Tess says, still laughing. "There's just something we have to do right now. Let's see if I remember how."

She stops the car on the flat shoulder of the road and hops out, waving for us. Grandpa Howe and I join her, not sure what's happening.

But Cassie won't budge. Grandma Tess pokes her head in the open driver's-side window and says something to her, while also turning up the stereo super loud. Cassie gets out, but not very happily.

"Okay, okay," Grandma Tess says, nodding her head up and down to the rhythm. "I think it goes like this. Watch, and we'll all do it together."

"Right here on the side of the road?" Cassie exclaims.

"Yes, darling." Grandma Tess ignores Cassie's pouty tone. "Right here in the road." Grandma Tess rocks her shoulders and begins to dance, not worried in the slightest, and I guess it's true we haven't seen many other cars.

"Step, step, step, step, then step, step, step, step, then back, and back, and up—stomp—step, kick and turn . . . You see? Clubs used to be full of people, all doing the Hustle together. Come on and try."

Grandpa Howe copies Grandma Tess, not caring much if he gets the steps right, so I stand as far back from the highway as I can and start following too. Cassie already thinks my life is stupid, so why not be more like Grandma Tess, and do the Hustle on a beautiful day in middle of the California desert when I've got the chance?

"Come on, Cassandra." Grandma Tess goes to where Cassie has been leaning against the hood of the car and takes her hands.

"This is dumb," I hear her say, though she does fall in beside us.

It doesn't take very long to get the steps down, and with Grandma Tess adding so much of her own style, it's impossible not to get groovy, too. I never took ballet or anything, and we don't have dances at my school, but sometimes when Mom and Dad have had a particularly stressful day, Dad will turn up the stereo really loud so that we can jump around and be silly while he cooks. Or we used to. We haven't done much of that in a while, since when Mom has her headaches we need to be quiet. So I stand out there in the desert under the blazing blue sky, and I dance as hard as I can.

As soon as the song is over, Cassie heads straight back to the car and her precious phone.

"Oh my." Grandma Tess sighs.

She and Grandpa Howe exchange a look. He takes her in his arms and kisses the top of her head. She lets herself melt into the hug for a minute, then gives Grandpa Howe a pat on his arm.

"Let me go talk to her," she says. "You two enjoy the view."

In truth, I want to go get my phone too, so I can tell Dad about what we just did, but it looks like being on the phone right now may not be a good idea. Instead I hook my arm around Grandpa Howe's waist and lean into him the way Grandma Tess was just doing. We stand there like that, watching the shadows of the fluffy clouds overhead chase each other across the camel-colored ground.

"That made me miss Dad," I say, to distract us both from the muted sounds of Grandma Tess and Cassie's fight behind us.

"It made me miss him too, Pumpkin. That kid always liked to shake his booty." Grandpa Howe chuckles and gets a faraway look. "Mostly what I want for my son these days is that he should be able to dance once in a while."

I wonder if Grandpa Howe's also thinking of Nana Lilia, and all the dance classes, trips, and volunteer work they'd planned to do when he retired. A couple of years before that time came, Nana Lilia got cancer, and Grandpa Howe decided to retire early. Only he ended up spending all that time taking care of her, and they didn't get to do everything else.

I know that for a long time after Nana Lilia died, Grandpa Howe's heart was broken. I knew this even though I was only ten at the time, and I hadn't understood how sick Nana Lilia was until suddenly Dad had to fly to Atlanta and then she wasn't here anymore. Around the first anniversary of Nana Lilia's death, though, Dad announced that Grandpa Howe was coming out to Berkeley to live closer to us. It took him a while to get oriented, and he was still sad sometimes, but pretty soon he started running into Grandma Tess at the yoga studio and the tea shop, and then, well, even though neither of them was really looking for it, something just clicked, and here we all are, dancing in the desert.

I hug him a little tighter, glad for him about Grandma Tess, but more because remembering Nana Lilia has made the fear about Mom shimmer awake in my stomach again. Dad and Mom were really sad when Nana Lilia told them about her diagnosis, and after that they talked a lot more with her and Grandpa Howe, but nobody had told me how bad it was. I hadn't known to worry about it, really, until Dad flew to Atlanta and then Nana Lilia was dead. Nobody wanted to scare me, I guess, but it also meant one day I had a grandma, and the next day I didn't. I can't help wondering now if the same thing is going to happen with my mom. I'm not little anymore, and I don't want to be in the dark in the same way again, even if I'm scared to know the truth. Or they're scared to tell me.

I'm trying to figure out a way to ask Grandpa Howe if there's more I need to know about all this stuff with Mom when we hear the car door open behind us. We turn as Grandma Tess stands and stretches, taking in a deep breath.

"That's settled, then." Her face is a little sorry, a little mad.

"Well then, let's go to Bakersfield." Grandpa Howe winks at me. "I hear the digs there are fantastic."

I swallow my questions for another time and squeeze Grandpa Howe's hand as we walk back to the car, preparing myself to have to sit next to Cassie and her rotten mood again. As I'm buckling up, I get a good look at her face. She's definitely been crying. I'd feel bad for her a little, but really, she's been asking for it. Grandma Tess starts up the car without a glance in the rearview at Cassie, who bends to get a small journal and a glittery pen from her bag. She writes what I assume are hate messages about Grandma Tess at first, but then she passes the notebook to me:

> *Nono took my phone for being on it too much.*
> *But Kendra Mack says Cory will text me any*
> *minute.*

Chapter Sixteen

Cassie

I thought my life was ruined when my best friend lost her diary, spilled my secret crush to the most popular girl at school, and revealed what she really thinks of me. I thought things were bad when, after I joined up with Kendra Mack, I got ignored one minute and tested the next by Izzy Gathing, and constantly teased by Gates Morrill and all his friends. I thought having to go on this awful trip with my grandmother and her new husband—plus my stupid stepcousin—instead of hanging out with my friends was the end of everything. I was wrong on all counts. Now my life is really, truly, absolutely, horribly *ruined*, and who do I have to blame? My favorite grandmother in the world—someone who's supposed to be excited for me in a moment like this but who has now single-handedly made this the absolute worst thing that has ever, and I mean ever, happened to me.

I hand my notebook over to Lana, and she almost doesn't take it, but when she does, her eyes go wide and I want to start crying again. The giant frowny face she draws on the paper doesn't come close to capturing how miserable I feel, though I'm relieved she's overlooking the awful things I said to her and isn't writing *I told you so*. Ugh, it's so terrible.

That Cory wanted my number is such a huge deal. And now, if Nono doesn't give me back my phone and I can't answer when he texts, he'll probably think I changed my mind and don't like him back. I'll have lost my chance.

We could try to explain and get it back. Just for a sec, Lana writes.

I take the pen from her. *She won't budge. I don't think she'll even let me use it to call my parents. She said I can use hers if I really need to.*

Lana's face twists in sympathy, but also thinking. She doesn't write anything for a minute. I stare out at the flat, nothing desert plain, not even able to listen to the saddest songs in my tune list. Instead I have to be assaulted by Nono's awful soundtrack of nostalgia.

I'll think of something, Lana writes. I can only hope she's right.

Lana tries to get me excited about the new hotel—which admittedly is pretty cool with its neon-lined reception counter and turquoise-and-mirror mosaic walls. Since I can't take any photos of it to send Kendra Mack or anyone else, though, I might as well not even be here. It's even dumb to bring in all my stuff, since I've decided I'm not dressing up for anything else on this whole trip, just to show Nono how mad I am. She thinks I express myself with my style? Well, just wait. Maybe I'll even wear the same jeans two days in a row.

As we walk through the chrome-and-white-leather lobby, Nono points out the announcement on the flat-screen by the elevators: *Welcome, Hayden and Rustoff families, for Nigel and Flora's wedding!*

"There's a wedding here tonight, Howie," she says, taking his arm.

"Well, we sure had a good time at ours," he replies.

"We sure did." Nono's eyes spark as she presses the up button for the elevator. "And we're going to have fun at Nigel and Flora's tonight!"

"How does she think we're even getting into a wedding we're not invited to?" I complain to Lana the minute we're in our room. "Why does everything have to be about her and whatever *she* wants? Could she stop and think of someone else for a second? Including, hello, a couple we've never met? What about their family? What about *us*? If we get kicked out, it'll be mortifying."

Lana hoists her duffel up on the rack in the closet and flops down on her bed across from me. She props her chin in her hands, frowning with concentration.

"Crashing a wedding is a little crazy, but I don't think that Grandma Tess is being selfish. She's doing this because she wants us to have a good time. All of us."

Immediately what Nono said to me when she took my phone jumps back in my mind: that it was her desire to share this exciting, loving time in her life with not just Howie—who she still keeps referring to as *Grandpa Howe*, as though that will magically make him my grandfather— but with me and Lana too. Apparently my texting makes her feel like I'm not really here. But if I have to share Nono with her new favorite husband and her new favorite granddaughter, I don't see why she can't share me with my friends.

"Why can't we just go to dinner and watch a movie or something here at the hotel?" I can't keep the whine out of my voice. "Why does everything have to be so—" *Crowded*, I want to say, though of course I can't to Lana. Really, the idea of sneaking into a fancy party with Nono sounds fun. It's just that now, of course, Howie will be there. And Lana. I'm surprised Nono's noticed I'm on my phone at all, since she loves them so much. Even if I'm upset, she just sings and dances the day away with them, not caring what's happening with me.

"Unpredictable," I finish.

"Maybe Grandma Tess feels we can watch movies and things like that all the time when we're at home," Lana says. "Maybe she wants to give us something special."

The horror of missing Cory's text crawls over me again. "If she wants to give me something special, she can give me back my phone," I grumble.

"Look." Lana folds into a cross-legged position in the middle of her bed, even though she still has her shoes on. "I know the phone thing is a really big deal. And I know you're really, really mad at Grandma Tess right now. But she's made up her mind, and you're not going to change it by sulking."

"I'm not sulking," I insist, wondering when Lana got to be such an expert on my Nono.

Her mouth twists in disapproval. "Well, you're not acting like someone who deserves to get your phone privileges back, either. By moping around and refusing to have fun, you're just proving to Grandma Tess that you *don't* want to be here, and that will make her way less likely to give it back."

I pound the bedspread with an angry fist. "I *don't* want to be here! Here I'm completely missing out on everything. I want to be back home, with my friends. And with my phone so I can talk to Cory!"

Lana stays calm. "I know that. But sometimes we don't get what we want. Sometimes . . ." She trails off, staring into space a second. She blinks, and her eyes snap back to focus on mine. "Sometimes you just have to be grownup even when it's not fair. Sometimes, when other people can't take care of you in the ways you think they should, *you* have to be the one to do it."

I raise my head off the bed to look at her straight on. There's something going on with her, it's clear. Maybe it's just my nosy nature, as Tom likes to point out constantly, but I want to find out what it is.

"Lana, when you said you'd tell me anything I wanted to know, did you mean—"

The hotel room phone rings so loud, Lana yelps. We look at it, then at each other, and both burst into nervous giggling. I watch as she says, "Hello?" and "Yes," and "Not yet," and "Okay, see you then" into the receiver, and gives me a kooky face as she hangs up.

"Grandma Tess says to be downstairs and glamorous in half an hour."

I groan, but I know Lana's right. This wedding-crashing thing is happening, whether I'm still mad at Nono or not. I can fret and watch the hours drag on and on, or I can take care of myself. If Nono's going to insist on doing what she wants, I'm at least going to do what I want within that. Which gives me an idea of how I can repay Lana for putting up with all this, too.

"We better get started then," I say. "I'm going to need every minute we've got to make you up proper for this wedding."

Chapter Seventeen

Lana

It felt like I was pep-talking myself more than Cassie when I told her that stuff about having to act grown-up when you don't want to, but I'm glad it worked for her. As soon as I'm off the phone with Grandma Tess, Cassie's plugging things in, draping outfits across the bed, checking what I've brought, and pulling out all her makeup—even the mantis-looking eyelash curler—preparing for my makeover.

"We'll have to be quick," she says, studying my face. "So it's a good thing you don't need too much done to you."

"I don't?" I ask.

Cassie makes a *duh* face that pleases me. "Look at your skin. You belong in an Ivory soap commercial. You should wear more than a ponytail all the time, though."

I reach up to grab the ponytail in question. "It always gets so tangled."

"I can help you manage it better."

I feel shy, being examined by Cassie so closely, but also delighted that she wants to share any of her expertise. It's good she doesn't think I need much makeup, though, because I definitely couldn't get into the kind of daily routine she has for herself. Besides, Tamika would have more than a thing or two to say about me wearing any of this silly stuff at all.

Cassie does us both up with some lavender-y metallic eye shadow, a tiny sweep of mascara, and tinted lip gloss that smells like cotton candy but tastes like overchewed gum.

"Now, your hair." She points for me to sit on the closed toilet lid.

I don't know what all she does—something with one of her heated instruments and some goopy-looking stuff in a tin—but when she tells me to turn around and look, I can't believe what I see. Instead of a mess of scraggy waves, my hair looks soft and pretty. Not as shiny as Cassie's, but still—nice.

"Here." Cassie hands me a wide floral ribbon. "Tie this around your head like a headband." She turns to examine herself in the mirror, sucking in her cheeks and looking left and right. "Now for me to figure out my mess."

Of course her hair isn't a mess; it's perfect. Well, mostly perfect, though it did get a little windblown while we were dancing on the roadside. She tries a few things as I watch from the toilet seat, but gets frustrated when she glances at the digital clock and sees we only have eight more minutes.

"Sometimes a bun is the best you can do," she says, pulling it all back.

"That should be Rule Number Eight," I laugh.

She sticks out her tongue. "Come on. We need to hurry and get dressed."

When the elevator doors open onto the lobby, Cassie and I hold hands and walk across the glossy floor over to Grandma Tess and Grandpa Howe.

"Why, you girls look so grown-up and lovely," Grandma Tess says, twisting her finger in a circle that says she wants us to spin around.

Even though Cassie complained about having "nothing" in her one solitary suitcase, she loaned me a flowered skirt that swoops all the way to the floor, and is wearing a beautiful sleeveless purple dress herself. We both feel pretty, and from the looks on our grandparents' faces, we know we are.

• • •

Getting into the wedding reception isn't nearly as hard as Cassie was afraid it might be. Grandma Tess simply puts her hand on Grandpa Howe's arm, ushers me and Cassie ahead of her, and smiles wide at everyone as we enter the beautiful rooftop deck. When a server offers us a tray, she lifts a little toast with pink stuff on it, grins with mischief, and says, "That Nigel always did have such great taste."

After we sample a little of the passed food, Grandpa Howe and Grandma Tess start dancing, so Cassie and I wander around the edge of the rooftop deck. When we find the macaroni and cheese bar, we heap our plates with varying types of cheesy deliciousness and head to a little corner where there aren't any other people.

"It's still weird, I think, going to a party where you're not invited," Cassie says around a mouthful of pasta. "But Nono's right. That Nigel has some very good taste."

I laugh in agreement.

"So, what's our plan?" she asks.

"Stuff ourselves with macaroni, I guess, and then maybe dance?"

She shakes her head. "About getting my phone from Nono. I have to see what Cory Baxter said. I just have to. And answer him real quick. Then I can put it back."

My happy mood starts to fizzle. Though I'd a little bit wanted Grandma Tess to take away Cassie's phone, I didn't want Cassie to actually miss out on talking to Cory. But I'd thought we'd just try asking for it back, or maybe working out a trade. Sneaking it from Grandma Tess would not only be hard to pull off, it'd be wrong.

"You wouldn't have to be the one to do it," Cassie says, seeing my hesitation. "I only need to get into her room. It's not like we're stealing, anyway, because it's *my* phone."

I look over at Grandma Tess and Grandpa Howe, dipping and twirling together on the dance floor. I want to change the subject like my dad does and make a joke about Grandma Tess teaching the whole wedding party the Hustle, but I know Cassie needs this. Needs *me*. I haven't ever broken the rules before, at least not on purpose. But this isn't about me—it's about Cassie, who needs my help.

A memory snaps into my mind: playing Civil War spy with Tamika in the park last summer. "Oh!" I say. "You could pretend to have a stomachache."

I tell Cassie about how Tamika (the spy) faked distemper in order to be admitted into the enemy's hospital. She did it so well that her brother Patrick (the general she was eventually going to steal the information from) almost called their mom at work, thinking Tamika was really sick. Maybe if Cassie faked a stomachache, we could get down to Grandpa Howe and Grandma Tess's room, where our trip first aid kit is. Grandpa Howe and I packed it with bandages, a snakebite kit, and various In Case medicines before we left, including Pepto-Bismol.

Cassie shudders. "Ugh, no. I hate throwing up." But then her eyes go wide. "A headache would be easy, though."

My heart shifts in my chest. I don't want Cassie making light of bad headaches—especially not to do something like steal back her phone.

"Maybe it's too obvious," I say, trying to change her mind.

"No, no." Cassie beams. "It's so simple it's brilliant. Let's do it!"

I slowly scrape the remaining sauce from my plate with the edge of my fork. The wad of cheese and pasta I just wolfed down is sitting inside me like a bunch of stones.

"Let's wait awhile," I stall. "It's less suspicious that way. In fact, we should probably do some dancing, maybe eat more than our share of those cupcakes over there in that tower."

Cassie nods, serious, and stands up. She holds out her hand to take mine and pulls me up beside her.

"Let's go, then, partner. We got plans."

Chapter Eighteen

Cassie

Lana's pretend headache idea is brilliant. Too bad it doesn't work. When we finish our macaroni, we go out on the dance floor. We jump up and down and shake ourselves silly, and a bunch of the groomsmen fake fight with each other to partner up with us, making Lana blush. When it's time for toasts, Nono and Howie are right in front, lifting champagne glasses with the parents of the bride. As usual, my Nono is the life of the party, and her crazy scheme has worked out beautifully. Maybe it's why I think getting back into her room will be so easy—as her granddaughter, I should be able to pull off crazy schemes, too.

But it turns out Nono and Grandpa Howe are *too* chummy with everyone.

After two super-chocolaty cupcakes and more punch, Lana's looking a little sick herself, but she can't turn down Howie when he comes over to twirl us on the dance floor.

Four songs later, I break away to find Nono. As I search the crowd, I hold my hand to my temple and try to make it shake a little. When I finally find her, she's laughing with a bunch of ladies by the photo booth, peering at a strip of pictures they just took together.

"What is it, darling?" She bends to get a better look at my face.

"I'm getting a headache," I say, making my voice as weak as possible. "Can I go see what we have in the first aid kit?"

"Oh dear," she says gently. And then—unbelievable—turns right to her gaggle of new girlfriends and asks if any of them have any pain medicine. Before I know it, there are six hands offering up different pills and powders.

"Thank you," I say, not having to fake my bad feeling anymore.

Nono leads me over to lie down on one of the loungers. She gets some water from a nearby waiter and wets a napkin to press across my brow before handing me the glass. She watches as I swallow down the pills, then takes my right hand and pinches, hard, in the place between my thumb and pointer finger.

"This pressure point usually helps me," she says. "It's been a lot of stimulation today, huh? Probably you haven't had enough water, either. Old Nono always forgets the basics, doesn't she?"

I sip the cool water to keep from answering, wondering what will happen to me now that I've taken those pills when there's nothing wrong with me at all.

"Everything okay?" Howie asks, coming over with Lana.

"A little too much exertion, I think." A wisp of guilt flickers in Nono's face.

"Do you need to go down—" Lana starts, but I interrupt.

"One of Nono's friends had some aspirin. I should be okay soon. You guys go on and enjoy the party. I just want to sit here a little bit."

"You sure you don't want to turn in?" Howie offers in a way I can tell is trying to be nice.

"You're having such a fun time, and I don't want to—"

"I might be a little tired too," Lana jumps in. "I'll go down to our room with you."

In her face I see she's doing this because she knows how terrible I feel about our failed mission, not out of any desire to stop dancing.

And maybe it's because the cupcakes, the pills, and

my phone still being on lockdown really are making me sick—or maybe it's the rush of gratitude I'm feeling for Lana—but I blink back real tears and nod to her. "Yes."

"I'm so sorry," Lana says as soon as we're alone together in our room.

I flop down on the bed, Lana-style, though I let my feet dangle over the edge.

"It doesn't matter to me anymore what we do on this trip. I might as well not show my face back at home," I say.

"We'll think of something," she says, though she sounds glum too. "Maybe you should take a bath. That always helps my mom relax when she . . . has a bad day."

"I don't want to move from this spot."

"Come on. I'll fill the tub for you. It'll feel good to soak your muscles."

She gets up, and soon there's water running in the bathroom. After a minute I hear her in there, talking. On her phone. Which she still has, and I don't. For a second I'm outraged. Of course *she* has her phone still. Perfect do-gooder just like Tom. I don't like her trying to hide it from me, either. I'm about to pound on the door, tell her she doesn't have to fake something nice like running a bath just to make a phone call, but my anger vanishes when I see the clock. It's only nine thirty—way too early for us to be down here getting ready for bed instead of having fun upstairs at the party. If it weren't for me, Lana'd still be up there having a blast.

Through the door I hear her say, "Love you too, Mom," and then it opens.

"I just had a thought. You can use my phone, if you need to. To call Kendra Mack."

"Thank you," I say, grateful and miserable and now feeling even worse, "but I don't know her number by heart."

Of course Fiona's number I still remember, because we memorized them together on the first day of sixth grade, when we got our own phones. But Kendra Mack, and Cory Baxter, and the rest of my existence are trapped in that phone.

My life is utterly ruined.

In the morning, party-hardy Howie and Nono call our room at eight thirty, not sounding the slightest bit tired. They're all giddy about taking me and Lana to Bakersfield's crowning glory, Camelot Park.

"I haven't been to an amusement park since I was, like, seven," I whine to Lana through the open bathroom door while I'm doing my hair. She's rummaging in her bag, and I can't help noticing the mess she's making. T-shirts and pairs of socks spill out around her.

"Trust me, it's better than the Crystal Palace, or the downtown walking tour that Grandpa Howe and I looked at. There's some cool history here, but not *that* cool. We picked out Camelot Park because we thought it would be *fun*."

I put my straightening iron down and stare at her. I'm not 100 percent sure, but Lana sounds mad at me. It gives me a surprisingly bad feeling.

"What are you looking for over there?"

"I could've sworn I packed my plaid cap in here somewhere, but I can't find it."

"I brought a baseball cap, if you want. It's pink."

"What I want is *my* cap." She leans back on her heels and pushes more things to the floor. Her voice is tense, impatient. "My mom got it for me, which makes it special, because she doesn't get me cute things very often."

Lana's level of anxiety about a hat seems a little excessive, but then I guess Nono thinks my involvement with my phone is excessive too. I cross the room and kneel next to her.

"Two sets of eyes are better than one, right?"

"I just could've sworn I had it in this side pocket." Her voice is elevating like she's on the edge of a temper tantrum. "So it wouldn't get smushed."

"Tom says usually whatever you 'could've sworn' is actually the opposite of what you did." I arch my neck, looking for her book tote. "What about in there?"

She gets up glumly and goes for it. When she looks in her book bag, she laughs.

"Right here," she says, holding it up.

I'm relieved to see her smiling. To help out, I start rolling her T-shirts up into tight little logs, putting everything back in her duffel so tidily that there's even room for more things on top.

"How'd you get to be so good at that?" she says, seeing what I've done.

I shrug. "My mom always says if I keep my things nice, it makes her more motivated to get me nice things. At this point it's mainly a habit. Your mom doesn't mind things being messy?"

A weird, stricken look crosses Lana's face, and she looks down at the cap in her hand. I feel like I've said something wrong.

"Lana, is everything okay?"

She doesn't lift her chin or her eyes. "My mom—"

I wait, but she closes her mouth and shakes her head.

There's a quick knock at the door: Howie and Nono, ready for our Big Day in Camelot.

Either finding her cap *really* turned her mood around (and I have to admit it's supercute on her), or Lana doesn't want

Howie and Nono knowing something's wrong. As we ride the elevator to the lobby, she pours on the eagerness extra thick. It's like she's trying to convince herself and the rest of the world that everything is fine.

"I think we should do the bumper boats first." Her voice is so *My Little Pony* high it makes my teeth hurt. "They have giant hoses on them that you can squirt each other with, so we'll have gotten soaked early but can dry off for the rest of it."

Nono suggests we do the wet stuff at the end, to cool us off, but I point out that would mean we'll be soaking on the drive back. Really I just don't want Lana starting up again.

"I don't mind what we do first," Howie says, "as long as it involves ice cream."

"You bet!" Lana says, practically pulling him to the car.

She is definitely hiding something, and I'm going to find out what it is.

After banana splits for breakfast, two and a half hours of mini golf (the line for the bumper boats was too long for it to be our first activity, Lana decided), plus Skee-Ball in the arcade and a basket of hand-cut potato chips smothered in gooey blue-cheese sauce, Lana seems a little more relaxed. She also, I noticed, sent a secretive text, and when she got an answer back quick, a lot of the tension went out of her face. Now we're leaning in together, smiling into Howie's camera. After the picture, Nono stands up and holds out her sticky hands.

"Time for me to take a mini bath, I think," she says. "You girls want to join me?"

She takes a step toward the bathrooms without reaching for her purse. Lana kicks me under the table. I realize this is my chance.

"I think I want to finish the rest of this," Lana says fast, gesturing to the basket. It's still soggy with a few fries and melty blue cheese at the bottom. "But we'll be behind you."

I nod in agreement, trying to think of how to distract Howie so that I can get into Nono's purse. As Nono strolls off, I say a silent prayer that there's a bumper-boat-length line in front of her.

Lana watches after Nono for a second, then dips two fingers around in the sauce and licks them off.

"That was excellent." She stands and wipes her hands on her shorts. I make a mental note to tell her that Rule Number Nine is Don't Be Disgusting. "We should scope out the go-karts," she says. "In case the line's long there, too."

"I don't think there's any harm in waiting for Tess," Howie says calmly.

I trade glances with Lana.

"But there's already people over there, see?" Lana points a greasy finger. Breaking Rule Number Three seems okay right now. "What if they're lined up around the back of the building?"

"I'll wait for Nono," I offer.

"Well, if you're that excited." He ruffles Lana's flyaway hair.

"You okay here?" Lana asks, giving me a thumbs-up behind her back.

"Nono won't be long." I wave them away.

Lana takes Howie's hand and beelines for the go-karts. As soon as they're a safe distance away, I plunge my hand into Nono's purse. I'll say I was looking for hand sanitizer if she catches me. It doesn't take much digging, because my phone's right there, in the narrow inside pocket. I jam it into my own purse and push Nono's a good arm's length away from me before I look up and see Nono dropping her paper towels into the trash just outside the restrooms. She waves, and I think she must immediately know what I've done.

"Lana was anxious about the go-karts," I explain coolly when she gets back. "I volunteered to watch our stuff."

"You're a sweetheart," she says. "Thanks for waiting. Let's go!"

She links her arm in mine and we skip toward the

go-karts, our steps bouncing high. When she smiles down at me, my smile is just as wide. It doesn't matter who beats me on that track, not even Howie. In the Keep Cassie Away from Her Phone game, Nono just lost.

Chapter Nineteen

Lana

I can tell from the way Cassie's beaming that she's got her phone back. Right away I'm nearly as excited as she must be to see what her messages are, but when I raise my eyebrows to her in a question, she shakes her head very slightly—*not yet*.

I can't say that I mind waiting, since it involves whipping around the go-kart track. Grandma Tess is in a neon-purple cart, me in fire-engine red, Cassie in a turquoise-blue one painted with ocean waves, and Grandpa Howe in a cart called "The Monster," with flames on the back and a big, toothy mouth on the front. In our first race, a big tattooed dad with a dark-blond beard wins overall, but Grandpa Howe comes in a victorious second, and Cassie and I aren't

153

far behind him. It's so much fun we immediately buy tickets for another round, and this time Grandma Tess pulls across the finish line first with both hands raised over her head.

"What's next?" she says, pushing her silver waves into non-flyaway shape.

Grandpa Howe suggests victory hot dogs, or at least something to drink.

"I need to let some things out before I put more in," Cassie says, glancing at me.

"I'll go with you," I add.

"You girls know where it is?" Grandma Tess has a tiny frown between her brows, and for a second I think she knows that our sudden need for the bathroom has nothing to do with toilets.

Grandpa Howe puts an arm around her, though, and turns her in the direction of the arcade. "I've got some Skee-Ball ticket winnings to cash in. Then we'll wrangle up some more snacks. What do you say?"

"Sounds great," Cassie and I both say at the same time, hard and fast. We look at each other and laugh nervously, and take off for the ladies' room.

"Ahhh, I can't do it." Cassie hands me her phone under the wall between our stalls. "You check."

"That's silly." I push her hand back with my foot and come out to wash my hands. Cassie lets me into her stall and we face each other, leaning on opposite walls. She didn't even have to go.

"What if he didn't text and this is for nothing?" She's still holding the phone but not turning it on.

"You're not going to know unless you do it." This is something Tamika's said to me more than once. "Just turn it on and find out." In my opinion, sometimes Tamika jumps into things without worrying about them enough, but I think Cassie's done plenty of worrying in the last twenty-four hours. "Here, I'll do it with you."

I hold my thumb over Cassie's and press her power button down, hard. We watch together as the screen blinks. Cassie's biting her lip, so I channel as much confidence as I think I'd need from a friend at a time like this. Soon enough, her phone *bleep*s five times, and Cassie's face lights up for a second, before it immediately pales.

"I can't look." She hands the phone to me. "At least tell me who they're from."

Her phone is fancier than mine, so I fumble a little to find the right icon.

"Two from Kendra Mack, it looks like. And three from"—I hold it out to her—"this number that you don't have a contact for."

"It's him," she squeals, grabbing the phone and bouncing up and down. "It's him, it's him, it's really him. I can't believe it."

"Well, what does he say?" We can't be in here too long, or Grandma Tess might come check on us, especially after Cassie's "headache" last night.

"Okay, okay." She stares into the screen, and I watch her face break into a slow smile, and a blush.

"The first one he says he's sorry he can't call, but that Izzy Gathing gave him my number and is it okay to text. The second one just says 'How are you doing?' Then Kendra Mack texted to ask what's up and how the trip is going. The most recent one is this morning, Cory asking does he have the right number, since he hadn't heard back from me. So cute. He's anxious too! I have to text him right back. What should I say?"

"Tell him you didn't have a signal until now. And that . . . I don't know, you're having fun?"

She starts thumbing the screen. "I should ask him a question too, right? To keep the conversation going?"

"Just remember to put that on silent if you're keeping it awhile," I warn her.

"Right, right." She's still typing. "I need to write Izzy Gathing and Kendra Mack too, to thank them and say what happened."

"I'll wait for you outside." I reach for the lock. "That way if Grandma Tess checks, she'll see I'm still waiting on you."

She stops typing long enough to grab me around the neck in a hug. "Thank you so much for being here with me," she gushes. "You are the best."

When Cassie comes out of the bathroom, the transformation is pretty remarkable. She hooks her arm in mine and skips us back into the arcade, where she suggests we try the driving game, since we didn't do so hot on the real-life go-kart track.

We duck inside the console, dark and enclosed like the inside of a real race car. Cassie drops in the quarters for a single round and goes back to her phone.

"Cory might text back," she explains. "I asked him what we should play, since he knows a lot about video games. That was smart, right?"

"Definitely," I answer, though a strange feeling creeps behind my shoulder blades. I wanted to help Cassie get her phone back to check it and send something quick to Cory, but I didn't think she'd hold on to it. If she gets chatting with him, not to mention with her friends about him, we'll be right back to where we were before—something I don't want for myself, but also for Grandma Tess and Grandpa Howe.

While Cassie texts and giggles and squeals in anticipation next to me, I crash three times in my race, and finally lose.

"Are you sure you should have the phone out like that?" I ask her. "Grandma Tess and Grandpa Howe might see."

Cassie shoves her head outside the race-car console.

"They're over there, at the basketball thing." She gestures with her head, and I stretch out to see Grandma Tess holding the ball while Grandpa Howe places his hands over hers, showing her just how to bend her wrist and press the ball forward. I wonder if he's told her any stories about when he used to coach his sons' elementary school basketball team. "They won't even see," Cassie says.

"Okay," I say, sinking into the driver's seat, still afraid they'll look over.

Cassie takes her time snapping a panoramic of the arcade. "Let's see what he thinks of this."

She sends it and sits there, happily watching the mock race on the screen and not moving.

"Want to play a round together while you wait?" I'm starting to get bored, and annoyed that Cassie wants to stop having fun just so she can wait for Cory to text her.

"I guess so." She puts her phone in her lap, with the screen facing up so she can still see if a message comes in.

Neither of us is very good, but Cassie blows up before

I'm even halfway done with the race. She watches, cheering me on, but her knee is jittering up and down, and I can tell she's not very into it. I think I liked things better when she didn't have her phone.

"How about some kind of shooting game?" I suggest. "Maybe that'll get out some of your frustrations."

"I'm not frustrated," she says coolly.

As we climb out of the race-car game, I can't help rolling my eyes. We pass Grandpa Howe and Grandma Tess at the basketball hoops and wave, before moving to the back of the arcade, where I spot one of those fantastic dancing games with a touch-sensitive floor. I remember the Hustle, and dancing at the wedding. Maybe a little dancing will bring Cassie back to the moment, and help me have fun, too.

"Come on, this is better than shooting," I say.

Cassie looks skeptical. "People are watching."

I turn in place, scanning the whole arcade. Besides Grandma Tess and Grandpa Howe at the hoops, there's one kid at the Whac-A-Mole, a couple of men in a serious game of foosball, and two little girls and their mom rolling balls up the Skee-Ball ramp and laughing as they roll back down.

"No one's watching. And even if they were, they'd just see us having fun." Fun the way Grandpa Howe's had since he moved to Berkeley, I think, and met Grandma Tess. Fun like I want my mom to have again. The kind you should have whenever you can, since there might not be another chance.

"Whatever," Cassie sighs, checking her phone again.

I stifle another eye roll, deciding if Cassie's not going to have fun, at least I will, and maybe she'll join me. I plunk in enough quarters, and as the music starts I ham it up, bending my knees and shimmying my hips the way Mom does when things really get groovy in our kitchen. Cassie stands there and gawks, and tells me to cut it out, which for some reason makes me want to do it more. I cross my eyes, flop out my tongue, and shift my head back and forth. I swivel my knees in opposite directions, then do my best to moonwalk as well as Dad can.

My game screen buzzes that I'm not following the moves right, so I switch for a minute to the easy jumps and kicks it wants me to. When I look over, Cassie's staring back at her phone. I wish I knew how to do back handsprings or something. Instead I start chopping at the air like one of Tamika's judo moves.

"You better get your groove on, Cassie Parker." I shift into Egyptian poses like the screen's telling me to do. "Hate to have to tell Cory Baxter what a loser you are on the dance floor."

Her head snaps up. "Those are fighting words, Lana Thorton-Howe."

I smile. "I know they are. He text you yet?"

She scowls. "No."

I rock forward and back, and kick, following the screen. "Well, this is a lot more fun than standing there looking desperate."

This makes her finally put her phone in her purse. "That's it. You're on."

She steps next to me with an intense look on her face and jumps into the moves even better than I was doing. We make it to round six together before we have to put in any more quarters.

But of course instead of going straight for her wallet, she goes straight for her phone. "Ooh, ooh! He wrote back! Four times!" she squeals. I plunge into my own quarter stash, so we don't lose out on the game.

"He says he doesn't know any of the games in my picture." Cassie frowns. "Don't you think that's weird?"

I plunk my change in the slot just in time. "Is what weird?"

"That he doesn't know these games? These other texts are goofy, too. Look—"

She holds out her phone, but I've had to start bouncing and twirling already, so it's too hard to see. "Read them to me," I say.

"He says he'd much rather play a game with me called

Who Takes the Grossest Selfie. He wants me to send him a picture with, like, my tongue out or something. Then he asks me who I think is uglier, Neftali Manji or Cheyenne Taylor."

"Ha," I say as she joins me on the floor, frowning.

After a series of quick turns in a row, and a bunch of high kicks that take fast footwork and concentration, Cassie says, "I'm not sure what I should say back to him."

"Say to whom?" Grandma Tess asks from behind us, startling us both. We pause, mid-bounce, and look at each other.

"We were just pretending," I say fast.

"Pretending we were at a real dance," Cassie adds.

"And what would we do if—if someone asked us to dance."

Cassie nods.

"Well, it would depend on what kind of dancer he is, right?" Grandma Tess says with a smile. The game starts counting down for us to add more quarters, but neither Cassie nor I make a move. "How does this thing work? It looks like fun."

"We can add you in, if you want," Cassie says. She still looks nervous.

"Howie should be in on this too." Grandma Tess

stretches up on her toes and waves him over from the change machine.

"Oh, I don't know about this," Grandpa Howe says when he arrives, peering at the screen while Grandma Tess pushes in enough quarters for all four of us to play. "Gonna need a good dance partner." To my surprise, he holds out his hand to Cassie.

Cassie glances at Grandma Tess a second, hesitating, but she raises her eyebrows at Grandpa Howe and takes his hand. "You better not make us lose," she teases. "Nono will be insufferable all afternoon."

He winks at her, and she smiles. Grandma Tess applauds and moves into position. "Lana, you stand in front so I can watch you and the screen. I already know how good you are."

Once again the music starts up, and the four of us hit it. Dancing in pairs is different from dancing individually— we get to do underhand turns, swerve in opposite directions, and this one part where we punch to the beat in alternate rhythms. Cassie and Grandpa Howe are pretty good, but he's not as coordinated as Grandma Tess, and we're winning. In the final countdown, right as it looks like they're going to lose, Grandpa Howe takes Cassie's hands, twirls her around, and somehow lifts her off the ground and spins her over in a flip. When she lands on two feet, her eyes and mouth are open in laughing surprise.

Grandma Tess and I are so shocked, we stop to clap, but Grandpa Howe and Cassie keep going and finish the dance. We end up losing by a single point, but it so doesn't matter.

"Hope that was okay," Grandpa Howe says to Cassie. "Just thought we needed to pull out all the stops there."

She gives him a high five. "So long as Nono doesn't get jealous."

"What Nono's getting," Grandma Tess says, clearly pleased, "is ready for some actual food. We haven't done the bumper boats yet, though, so what do you say we head for our big final splash, dry off in the sunshine, and then see what downtown Bakersfield has to offer in the dining department? I may have had my fill of amusement park junk."

"Cool," Cassie says, picking up her purse. I notice she slides her hand inside it, probably to make sure her phone's still there, or to feel it if it buzzes.

As we fall into step behind our grandparents, she sneaks me a *Wow, that was close* look. While I'm glad we didn't get caught—and the whole dancing thing was a heap of fun—part of me still can't wait to drench her with a Super Soaker.

Chapter Twenty

Cassie

For our late lunch Howie finds the hands-down weirdest place. Instead of quiet little booths, the family restaurant called Noriega's has long, giant tables stretching across the room, and everyone sits together. Worse than sitting with strangers? We can't even pick what we eat. Instead the old-lady waitresses bring out huge platters of food, and we all help ourselves family-style to the beans, soup, salad, bread, and bleccch—thin slices of cow tongue. Ugh.

"This place is certified Basque at its finest," Howie says happily, swallowing a bite of tongue and scooping up some bean sauce with a chunk of bread. "Not to mention highly rated by James Beard."

Lana and I swap a look that says we just don't want our lunches licking us back.

"Makes me miss the commune days, I'll admit," Nono says. "Sharing meals together was one of my favorite parts."

"Sure you weren't too busy painting to make it to dinner?" Howie teases her.

Nono protests with a laugh, explaining that she actually had a very strict studying schedule, so that she could finish her college education in three years. The fun around the table was her only break.

"I will say I bartered to get out of my chores as often as I could," she tells us. "At one point I owed three chakric crystal readings, two healing-touch massages, and my favorite Guatemalan poncho."

"You know how to read crystals?" Lana looks at Nono with the same admiration I always feel when Nono tells stories. I get a flash of pride at how awesome my grandmother is. It's nice in the same way as when on one of Nono's visits, she treated Fiona and me to pedicures, and the two of them immediately clicked. Something like that will never happen again, of course. Kendra Mack and my other new friends would not be impressed by Nono's hippie stories, either. I'm glad Lana loves them, though.

Nono explains how her debts to everyone were eventually what led to her friendship with my mom's birth father,

Richard Hsu. The story is especially fun for me, since I already know Nono's punch line. I squeal out, "She doesn't read them at all!" right as Nono says, "I don't know the first thing about them," and we all crack up.

Back at the hotel, the receptionist hands Lana a postcard: a picture of two old-fashioned cowgirls whipping lassos over their heads. Lana reads it as we head to our room, where we have about an hour to pack our things and get ready for driving on to Modesto. Modesto means heading back north, and only a couple more days of the trip. Not that I'm sorry. I just didn't expect time to fly by so fast.

Hopefully in that hour I'll think of how to reply to Cory's weird texts, since I can't stall much longer before answering him.

"What does Tamika say?" I ask Lana.

"Oh, not much. She's telling me about all the cool stuff she signed up for at Wilderness Camp, and that so far she likes all her cabinmates."

"You should tell her about all the things *we've* done. Way better than sleeping in a smelly tent and having to cook beans over a fire, if you ask me."

Lana laughs out her nose. I start wrapping the cord for my hair straightener, letting memories of the trip so far drift through my mind. I'd thought this was going to be an awful week, and there have certainly been some bad spots, but I'm a little sorry it's almost over.

My phone vibrates, and Kendra Mack pulls me back to reality:

Cory Baxter wants to know *for sure* if you are coming to my party Saturday. Hope it's okay that I invited him!

I nearly scream with happiness, texting her back, OF COURSE!!

"Kendra Mack invited Cory Baxter to her pool party this weekend!" I say as I'm typing. "And he wants to make *sure* I'm going to be there."

Lana's eyebrows come together. "He wasn't invited before?"

I'd forgotten that Lana still thinks Cory is my real boyfriend. I wish I'd never told that stupid story at Nono and Howie's wedding. It's hard to keep track of who knows what, and it feels weird now, Lana not knowing the truth. One more quick lie is easier than explaining the whole thing, though.

"Kendra Mack's mother doesn't like to invite over people she's never met before." It sounds like it could be true. "Apparently Kendra Mack's been begging all this time. And now, he'll be there!"

The idea makes me giddy. I snatch up my phone and

snap a quick selfie with my eyes crossed and my tongue peeking out, since Cory'd asked for one earlier. With it I text: **I really hope you'll be able to make Kendra Mack's party.** It's more a silly shot than gross, but I hope he'll think it's cute and text me a cute one back.

I switch over to my playlist and search for one of my favorite songs. "Come on," I tell Lana. "We need a celebration dance."

"You didn't get enough of that at the arcade?" she says.

"Not to this I didn't," I say, turning up the volume as loud as it goes. I grab Lana's hands. "And not on cushy hotel beds!"

I pull her up and start bopping around to the music. She gives in, and soon we're yelling the lyrics and bouncing together, until we stumble on the comforter and collapse into laughs.

"We're more than halfway through the trip," Lana pants, as the song winds down. She's on her back, looking at the ceiling, with her feet raised over her head.

I roll over onto my elbow. "I was thinking about that too."

The edge of her mouth twists. "You probably can't wait to get back, though."

"No, I can't wait," I admit. "But this has been way more fun than I expected. Besides, I bet Tamika's got big plans for once you're both home."

Picturing Lana and Tamika comparing notes about their time apart makes me feel a little sad, actually. No one in my group will want to know about giving silly names to exotic pets, or Dessert First, or Howie's slick swing-dance move.

Lana nods and turns her face away. "Can Rule Number Ten be that we promise to still talk to each other, even when we're back at home?" she asks quietly.

I pause. It's nice being with Lana now, but she'd never fit in with my group, so it's hard to imagine her fitting into my real life. I certainly wouldn't talk to her instead of Kendra Mack. The idea of texts streaming in from Lana while I'm with my friends or Cory Baxter feels awkward too. I nudge her with my foot. "You can call me if you want sometime. We don't have to make a rule about it."

She keeps looking away. "You'll have a lot going on, with Cory and everyone, I guess. I just thought it might be reassuring. That, you know, you won't forget about me."

I feel weird, talking about this. I can't make a promise to Lana that I know I can't—and likely won't want to—keep.

"I'll probably be texting you after Kendra Mack's party," I dodge. "So you can help me laugh over whatever stupid thing I manage to do in front of everyone."

She finally meets my eyes. "You're not going to do anything stupid."

I'm saved by a *bing* from my phone. There's another message from Cory: **Can't wait gorgeuz you are so prettee. Kendra Mack sez u are even sweeter than you look. Is that true?**

My stomach drops. It's hard to tell if he's joking about my selfie and I'm not quite getting what's funny, or if he really talks like that. Either way, it doesn't match at all what I thought I knew of him. I have no idea why he's being so bizarre. Or why he's also texting with Kendra Mack. I tell him I have another excursion to head off to and I'll talk to him later, and put my phone in my purse. There's packing to finish.

I decide that having to keep my phone hidden from Nono is a good thing, if Cory's going to be so weird. Once we're back in the car, Howie tells another story about the End of the Road, and the summer carnivals in town there every year. It's old-fashioned, but the way he describes the Ferris wheel and seeing a cotton candy machine for the first time is cute. Nono's got some quiet music playing, and Lana's harmonic humming is soothing instead of irritating. She really does have a good voice. I'm admiring the pretty farmland we're passing and wondering what our evening will be like when there's the most awful sound: my phone, chiming in with a text.

I freeze. Next to me, Lana stiffens too. I'm hoping that the music has kept Nono from hearing, but then it chimes again, and she looks back in the rearview mirror.

"Lana? Is that your folks?" she asks.

"Um—" Lana reaches down for her bag.

As she's pretending to look for a text that isn't there, the ring tone I use for my dad discos loud and jarring from beneath my feet.

Nono sighs. "I suppose you'd better answer it, Cassandra."

I don't want to move, but if I don't answer, Dad'll just hang up and send me a billion texts, which will only make it worse.

"Hi, Dad," I say, feeling the horrible glow of the phone against my cheek.

"We just got the Labor Day party goods out of the attic," he tells me. "But we're going to wait for you to help decorate and do the shopping."

"Is that so?" I say, though I can barely speak.

He keeps talking, and I feel words like "I think so" and "It'll be fun" coming from my mouth. I'm aware of the whole car listening to my conversation. This conversation I shouldn't be having, because I shouldn't have my phone.

Dad asks if he can say hey to Nono. "She's driving," I try, but Nono's already reaching her hand back to take it.

To say I want to throw up or leap out of the car doesn't

even cover it. I can feel Lana looking at me, but I keep my eyes straight ahead on the back of Nono's seat as she pulls over and tells my dad where we are, where we'll be staying, and that no, we girls aren't wearing her and Howie out too much.

She should be laughing, joking with my dad, but her voice is dead serious.

"Cassie and I will have a few things to discuss together when we get to Modesto, though, I think." She pauses, and I can hear my dad asking a question but not the words. "No, I'm sure it'll be fine. No trouble we can't handle," she says.

At least Nono isn't telling Dad what I've done. If he knew I'd stolen from my own grandmother, I'd probably be banished to my room for the rest of my life. Kendra Mack's party would be out of the question.

Nono listens for another minute. "Well, perhaps we should count this as our check-in right now, and you can tell Serena I'll call her tomorrow at our regular time."

That Nono's been talking with Mom every day surprises me, but I guess it shouldn't. Mom is very regimented. If Nono tells Mom about this phone business, it's going to be hideous. But not as hideous as the horrible feeling that Nono knows I've betrayed her.

Nono ends the call and hands my phone back to me.

"You'll turn that off now, please," she says. "I still have some decisions to make."

"Okay," is all I can answer.

Nono doesn't say a word about it the rest of the way to Modesto. She taps her fingers on the steering wheel to the nostalgia playlist, and when her favorite Stevie Wonder song comes on, she sings at the top of her lungs. Like nothing has happened. Like I'm not going to be in a pile of trouble when she finally talks to me about it.

Chapter Twenty-One

Lana

"Be ready for a walk and then dinner in five minutes," Grandma Tess says as soon as the hotel elevator opens onto our floor.

Cassie looks like she's swallowed a live frog, or worse. I'm not sure if she'll even be able to eat. I can imagine all the terrible things that must be going on in her head, and Grandma Tess being mad at her is only the tip of the iceberg.

When Cassie's phone made that first noise and Grandma Tess thought the text might be mine, I had no idea what to do. I didn't want to lie to Grandma Tess, but I didn't want Cassie to get caught, either. When the phone finally rang so clear at Cassie's feet, I admit my relief felt bigger than my horror. Still, this is all unpleasant, and Cassie and I don't even have time to talk about it.

In our ahead-of-time research, Grandpa Howe and I chose a few possible spots around town for dinner, but somehow without discussion, we all know this needs to be Grandma Tess's decision. She marches ahead of the three of us, taking big strides in her Chacos and capris, her batik bag banging against her hip with every step.

I've never seen Grandma Tess so angry before. Well, not angry at a person. Last year during election season she went on a rant about "self-aggrandizing positioning," which Dad explained came from the frustrations she faced when she served as county commissioner years ago, but that anger lasted for about ten seconds and ended in a resigned laugh. This angry is the kind my mom can get—the kind that won't talk to you all day, and will only give you a good-night kiss out of a sense of duty. Personally, I prefer my dad's form of getting upset. He may throw giant temper tantrums that sometimes involve lots of yelling and even frustrated tears on his part, but his anger always passes quickly, and if you can stay calm through it, when it's over, it's like nothing happened.

Not even Grandpa Howe can pretend this angry isn't happening, though. He walks between Cassie and me, holding hands with us and keeping a small distance from

Grandma Tess so she can have space for whatever feel-ings she needs to. I'm glad Cassie's letting Grandpa Howe give her some comfort, because I know she needs it. He might've actually gotten some practice with this kind of thing from dealing with my dad.

Grandma Tess is right to be mad at Cassie, of course, but what she doesn't know is that she should also be upset with *me*. I'm the one who put the idea about getting the phone back in Cassie's mind, and I tricked Grandpa Howe into getting in the go-kart line with me so she could take it out of Grandma Tess's purse. At the very least, I should've tried harder to keep Cassie from doing it at all, or made her put the phone back after responding to Cory's first batch of texts. All I want to do is tell Grandma Tess how sorry I am, and that it's my fault too. But bringing it all up again might get Cassie in even bigger trouble.

After a while of walking in silence, Grandma Tess picks a Mexican place with a giant sombrero on the roof and cacti in terra-cotta pots decorating the open-air patio. "Tell us about your mail from earlier today, Lana," she says when we're seated. She has a tight smile on her face, but I can tell she's trying to loosen it.

"Oh. It was from Tamika." Making regular conversation feels hard. "She sounds pretty excited about camp."

Grandma Tess makes an expression like this might be

the most interesting thing she's heard all day, so I go on and explain what Tamika is doing at Wilderness Camp. The whole time I'm aware of Cassie in the chair beside me, leaning hard against her own hand, like the thought of keeping her head up without support is far too much.

Grandpa Howe throws in a story about "roughing it" at the End of the Road one Christmas when an ice storm took out the power for a few days. Since we don't have severe winters in Berkeley, it all sounds intense and a little scary, but the way Grandpa Howe describes his mother trying to finish baking their Christmas cookies in the fireplace is funny. Cassie's obviously not listening, though, and the whole time Grandma Tess casts disapproving glances in her direction. We even forget to order dessert first.

It's not a long walk back to the hotel, but every step still feels heavy. Grandma Tess hasn't mentioned Cassie's phone, but we all know she's going to.

"Time for Cassie and me to have a conversation," Grandma Tess says when we reach the hotel lobby. "What do you think? On the patio there?" She gestures to the sliding glass doors as though Cassie has a choice.

"Grandma Tess, I—" I start, but Cassie immediately shoots me a silencing look, cutting off my confession. "I'll write Tamika back," I say instead, to let Cassie know I'll be waiting.

"And I've got a good book to tuck into, myself," Grandpa Howe says.

"Wonderful." Grandma Tess puts her hand on Cassie's shoulder.

From the way I feel and from Cassie's expression, I know it is just the opposite.

As soon as I get back to the room, I call Mom and Dad. I haven't heard from them since I texted that we were on the road to Modesto several hours ago. I know Dad always says, "No news is good news," but my gut feels like no news is bad news, and I need to check in.

When Dad answers, he tells me to call back on video chat. Mom's there beside him, looking pretty tired. While we talk, I watch her carefully for signs of more pain, but the screen is small and it's hard to tell much with her laughing over my stories about go-karts and bumper boats. Dad keeps the chat short, pretending to be the exhausted one so that Mom doesn't have to say she is, but when we hang up, they're both smiling. Still, I'm glad I'll be home before too long, where I can keep a closer eye on things.

Cassie's still not back, so I write Tamika another postcard. I consider telling her something about how unsettled

I'm feeling about Mom, but a postcard isn't that private, and who knows who might see it. I decide to stick to the fun stuff.

I've washed my face and just barely finished changing into my pajamas when Cassie lets herself back into the room.

"What happened?" I ask right away.

She shrugs, sad and defeated. "She took my phone. Permanently. I can't have it back until the end of the trip."

I was expecting that, though, and it's not really much longer.

"What else did she say?"

Cassie lifts her hand as though there's no point in explaining. She sighs and drops onto the bed. "She said the things you'd think she'd say. That she's disappointed. That she thought she'd explained you all want me here, with you, not distracted by people at home. She said sometimes being away from your friends makes it better when you're back, which, hello, *no*. Maybe knowing her friends' details isn't important to her, but it's important to me." Tears crest over Cassie's lower lids, and her shoulders start to shake. "It's so important."

I glance over my postcard to Tamika, not sure it *has* to be as important as Cassie imagines. Tamika and I said good-bye in her driveway two days before I left, and when I get back, she'll still be gone for two weeks. I miss her, but our friendship isn't at stake or anything.

"I'm sure Kendra Mack will fill you in on everything you missed. Even Cory will—"

"No!" she wails. Two giant tears drop down her cheeks. "I have to keep up with them. I *have* to. If I don't stay in touch, it won't matter when I get back. If you miss out on something with them, you're out. I'll be nobody and I'll have nobody."

I reach out, tentatively, and touch her knee. "Cassie, you'll always have me."

"That's not what I'm worried about." She groans, flopping into the pillows. "You don't get it. You're not there, with Tom and his perfect grades and his million friends, everyone comparing us all the time. You don't have the same life I do. You just don't."

Maybe this would be a time to tell her that my life isn't near as perfect as she assumes, but she starts crying harder, and it breaks my heart. She's right that I don't know what it's like to have a big brother to compete with, or demanding friends who tease and judge you, but I do know how to do what's right.

"I need to talk to Grandma Tess," I say, standing up.

"But first I'm running you a hot bath."

"It won't make a difference," Cassie moans into her pillow.

"Maybe not in a big way," I tell her, just like Mom tells me, "but small things can still help. Plus, there's a super-good-smelling thing of bubble bath in there. I checked everything out while you were gone."

Without waiting for another word from her, I turn on the taps in the bathtub, test the temperature, and pour in the soap, and head down the hall to my grandparents' room.

"Lana," Grandma Tess says when she answers the door, looking a little concerned and mostly plain tired. "Is everything all right?"

"No, it isn't," I say. I keep my hands in little fists by my sides, to help me feel brave. "I don't think it's fair for you to punish just Cassie. I need to tell you that I helped, too."

Grandma Tess opens the door wider. Inside, Grandpa Howe is sitting in one of the armchairs reading something on his tablet, his glasses pushed far down on his nose.

"Hey there, Pumpkin," he says. "Something you want to talk about?"

Grandma Tess sits in the chair across from Grandpa Howe and tucks one leg under her body. Thinking of Mom, and how she's always taught me to amend a wrong as soon as you learn about it—even just a miscommunication—I plunge forward.

"I just want you to know that this isn't all Cassie's fault. It was my idea to try to get her phone back, and I helped her do it. Grandpa Howe"—I turn to him, not sure I can look him square in the face—"I tricked you into getting into the go-kart line yesterday, when Grandma Tess went to wash her hands, so we could leave Cassie alone with the purse."

He's watching me over the top of his glasses. "Was there a reason?"

I swallow, hard. "Cassie was having an important conversation. And I wanted her to feel like she could rely on me if she needed help with something."

Grandma Tess's eyebrows shoot up, and she looks like she's about to launch into a lecture. Grandpa Howe clears his throat in a small, almost undetectable way, but it's enough to stop her. I'm grateful, because Grandma Tess's frustration makes me feel even worse than watching Cassie cry in our room.

"I know you're disappointed," I go on, even though my throat is clogging up and my eyes feel funny. "And I know it was wrong to lie to you. I was just trying to be a friend to her. I'm sorry."

"Well," Grandpa Howe starts, "I don't see how—"

But this time Grandma Tess stretches her fingertips out, just slightly, wanting to interrupt.

"I appreciate your coming to us, Lana, and I accept your apology. But, you know, this isn't so much about Cassie sneaking her phone back, but about how she acts as though she cares more about the people on the other end of it than the ones she's with."

"That's not true," I blurt, even though I've felt the exact same way. "Her friends at home, they aren't as understanding as we are. And I think that's what she needs right now. For someone to understand."

It isn't a full explanation, and I'm feeling all flustery, but I must say something right in there, because Grandma Tess's face immediately softens.

"Thank you, Lana," she says. "I'm glad for Cassie that she's got a friend like you on her side. And don't worry, I'm keeping her phone but not my anger. I fully intend for this to blow past us while we sleep and to keep having fun in the time we have left." Her eyes regain a little of their usual warmth. "I'm not interested in doling out unnecessary punishments, and I think putting up with everything tonight is all the hardship you need around the issue."

I nod, the funny feeling in my throat getting even wobblier. I've never had to talk to Grandma Tess like this before, and it surprises me how much her rational explanations remind me of Mom's. It's comforting, but it also makes me wonder if this quality of Grandma Tess's will be a too-hard thing to be around once my mom isn't anymore.

"I understand," I say, barely able to whisper.

"Let's all get some rest." Grandma Tess straightens up to stretch her back. "Tomorrow we'll be together again. Okay?"

I nod, crossing to give her a good-night hug, and one to Grandpa Howe. When I feel his strong hands against my back, I let myself collapse into the spicy-sweet scent of him, the linen-and-sunshine feel of his skin. If it weren't so late, and everyone weren't so tired, I'd curl up right here and finally talk to him about everything.

"You're a good girl, Pumpkin," he murmurs into my ear.

I nod against his cheek, because I can't do anything else.

"But we've got some standards to uphold around Dessert First tomorrow," he says, pointing a finger at me when I let go. "We slacked a little today, I think."

I eke out a small smile, but I know no amount of dessert tomorrow, or for the rest of this trip, will sweeten away the bitter fear inside me.

Chapter Twenty-Two

Cassie

It's Lana who wakes me up in the morning, instead of my alarm, since I don't have my phone anymore. I have no interest in getting up, though. She fumbles around for probably fifteen minutes before I even turn over.

"You can have the shower first," I say.

She pauses. "You sure?"

"I just want to lie here anyhow." I don't see the point in looking good when I can't send out pictures anyway. If Kendra Mack isn't watching, it doesn't matter what I do.

All I care about now is getting *home*. Well, that and finding out what Kendra Mack has been texting to Cory, and why he's being so weird.

When Lana gets out, she stands at the edge of my bed and pokes me.

"I've got another rule," she says.

"What is that?"

"We've only got two more days to make this vacation truly unforgettable, and I say we really apply ourselves. The rule is, We Are Going to Make This the Best Trip Ever, No Matter What. Deal?"

I sit up and drag my feet over the edge of the bed. "I'm not sure how we're going to do that, exactly."

"Go in there, get yourself cleaned up, and let's think about how to have some serious fun today, okay?" She grabs me by the shoulders. "Good. Times. I mean it."

"Okay," I grumble, dragging toward the bathroom. But I appreciate Lana's straightforward determination. Last night, when she told me everything she'd said to Nono and Howie, it surprised me that she was so honest. For my sake. If the tables had been turned, I probably would've faked innocence to avoid any extra wrath that might spill over, but not Lana. It's nice, too, to be with someone who tries to make a good time out of something less than great. My friends now are always trying to outcomplain each other. I guess I'd forgotten what it's like hanging out with an upbeat person. And Lana's right. I *can* try harder to make the best out of this time. If not for my own sake, then for hers.

To my surprise, deciding to feel better *does* feel better, and as soon as I finish my shower I go straight for the little desk between our two beds. There's a brochure I remember seeing.

"What do you think?" I hold it up for Lana.

It takes her a second to process the red-and-yellow lettering, but then she breaks into one of those adorable dimply grins.

"*River* rafting? Are you sure?" she says.

I smile as huge as I can. "You're good at the pep talks, what can I say?"

When we meet Nono and Howie in the lobby, they both hug me like nothing ever happened. I'm so determined to follow Lana's new rule that I even hug Howie back. I can tell Nono's expecting me to still be mad at her, but she relaxes when Lana and I start squealing about rafting and shove the brochure at them.

"That's not one I'd considered." Nono laughs. "Howie, what do you think?"

He pretends to frown with uncertainty, opening the splashy brochure to examine the information on the inside.

"Well," he drawls. "Sounds a heap better than the historical car museum, if you ask me."

Lana and I high-five each other, and we all decide to go for the hotel's continental breakfast, so we can get going and catch one of the first rafting tours.

"You two make quite a duo," Nono says when we sit down. "I'm going to miss this energy when the trip's over. I wish there wasn't such a distance between our houses. It'd be nice if we could all be together like this more often."

"Well, you never know what might happen," Howie says, spreading a thin layer of butter on his bagel. "In fact, I know a place where such a wish could be made, and granted."

Lana wiggles in her seat next to me. "This is a good story."

"Let me guess," I say, trying not to roll my eyes, "the End of the Road?"

Howie taps the side of his nose and smiles. "It's very difficult to predict exactly when, but there's a special night around the end of August there, when the entire peninsula is transformed by magic. Now, I see you not believing me, Miss Cassie, but it's not just some old wives' tale told by the ladies at the country store. I've experienced it myself— a night when fairies dance, mermaids sing, elves drum, tree sprites laugh, and wishes come true."

"I don't believe I've quite heard this version," Nono says.

Howie's eyes crinkle. "Well, I can't share this story with just anyone."

"Tell them what you have to do on that night," Lana says. She's practically vibrating, but Howie's right, I don't believe him. Nobody over the age of five believes in fairies. Certainly not in laughing trees.

"It is possible to harness all this swirling magic and make a special wish," he goes on, "but your timing has to be impeccable. For a wish to come true, you must skip a stone exactly seven times across a smooth ocean shimmering with phosphorescence, and fireflies glinting above its surface. Skip the stone, catch one of these fireflies, release it, and look up to find your falling star. A wish made on that star, if you've done everything just so, always comes true."

Nono leans back in her chair and crosses her arms. "That's quite a pile of requirements." I'm glad she sounds skeptical, too.

"No!" Lana blurts. "It's true! Tell them."

"It sounds far-fetched," Howie agrees, "but the summer I was nineteen, there was a beautiful, tough snap of a girl I'd met at the town clambake just a couple of weeks before. I couldn't do one thing right to get her attention, though. Every time I asked her to join me for a movie or an afternoon in the boat, she'd turn me down flat. She was on my mind when my brothers and I went for an evening walk to the ocean. There was something different in the air—we all felt it—and Tad dared me to try for the seven skips of the legend. It took a few attempts, but I made it, and sure enough the water lit up, fireflies swirled from nowhere, and a star streaked across the sky right above us. I wasn't sure I really believed in the magic, but I did think of Lilia, and how I wished to have one more chance with her."

Lana keeps grinning as Howie tells us how the very next day, he and his mother ran into Lilia at the grocery store, and Lilia smiled at him in a way he'd never seen before. He'd caught sight of a poster for a band performance at the gazebo that weekend, and right there he asked if she'd be willing to join him.

"Is *that* how your first date with her happened?" Nono gasps, looking delighted.

Howie pops a bite of bagel in his mouth instead of answering, and carefully wipes his fingers. Lana's about to burst, but in my opinion Howie's laying it on a little thick.

"Seven weeks later, I asked that girl to be my bride," he finally says, leaning over like he's whispering to me in confidence. "She happened to say yes."

"That's not all, though," Lana takes over. "Mom and Dad did the Magic Moment too. A few summers after they were married, and the whole family was up there together, my parents went out to see if Grandpa Howe's stories might be true."

"I didn't think Peter could manage the stone skipping, to be honest," Howie tells us, "but nine months later, we had Lana."

An outrageous blush flares across my face. I'm pretty sure Lana's parents may have been doing something other than skipping stones out there. Lana's so cute, though, I decide to never say a thing to ruin this story for her, even if it is silly.

"I tried again myself a few years ago," Howie goes on, "when I went up to get things going on the sale of the house. That was right after we'd gotten the results from Lilia's biopsy. But I guess my timing wasn't right."

The shine has gone from Howie's eyes, and Nono squeezes his hand. "Remind me why you sold the End of the Road?" she says.

Howie explains that after Lilia's cancer diagnosis, it was clear he'd need to be focused in Atlanta for a while. His brother Buck was gone by then, and Tad felt he couldn't manage the property with all his international business travel. Tad's daughter was firmly entrenched in New York, and Howie's own children were far-flung across the country, raising families. Lilia and Howie wanted the house to be lived in and appreciated, not sitting empty, so they decided to sell.

"Of course, at that time," he goes on, "we thought there'd be plenty more wonderful vacations to come, but we had our sights set on more exotic places than the End of the Road."

I'd never heard any of this about Howie's first wife. Though I'm glad Nono and Howie found each other, it's still sad to think about. The whole wishing thing might be ridiculous, but I can understand that it was a really special place for him.

"Well, *I've* always thought the End of the Road sounds exotic," Nono says, rubbing the tablecloth on either side of her plate. "In fact, I want to see it."

"I'll take you out there one summer," Howie says. "Maybe the new owners will even let us rent it."

"No." Nono's voice has a firmness in it that starts a terrible feeling in my stomach. "I think we should go see it right now. Why, it's almost the end of August as we speak. If we head out this morning, we'll be there in a few days. Then we could *all* catch the Magic Moment, and I can't possibly think of a more beautiful way to cap off this trip and begin our new life together. Not to mention get my wish about us all living closer. I bet at least one of you has a big wish of your own to make, too. Come on, girls"—she pushes her chair back and stands up—"let's call your parents and get our things."

"Really?!" Lana says, looking back and forth between Nono and Howie like they just told us we're moving to the moon.

"But I can't!" I cut in. Panic makes everything at the table look sharp. "I have something to do on Saturday. It can't be rescheduled, and I absolutely can't miss it."

"Whatever could be so important?" Nono asks. She's not questioning me in that way grown-ups do when you think something's vital but they don't. She genuinely wants to know. But I also know that Kendra Mack's pool party isn't going to be a good enough answer. Not even Cory Baxter is, because as much as Nono believes in love, she also thinks I'm too young for it. I search my brain for a lie good enough to keep Nono from dragging me across the country thanks to one of Howie's dumb stories, but I know if there was anything truly serious on Saturday, like a funeral or a wedding, Mom and Dad would have already told her about it.

"It's . . . my friend . . . she's . . ."

"Yes?"

I want to say "in the hospital," but I know that's not anything to lie about, either. Besides, lying in front of honest Lana feels weird. My heart sinks, and with it sinks my voice. "She's having a really big party is all. Everyone's going to be there, and if I miss it . . ."

"You'll still be back for your family's Labor Day gathering," Nono reasons. "Plus, you'll be with your friends every day once school starts. Who knows when you and Lana will see each other next? Or us, for that matter. Besides, I'd far rather rocket across the country with three people I love, to experience one of the most special events I'd ever heard of, than hang around at some party. Wouldn't you?"

Nono's not being mean about it. She honestly thinks that being stuck in the car for another week, maybe more, with her, Howie, and Lana to go stand in the dark, looking for shooting stars and making stupid wishes that will never come true, would be better than Kendra Mack's party. Or the chance to finally talk to the boy I've been crushing on for months. She honestly believes that. So there's no point—no point—in trying to explain.

"I guess so," I say, unable to look at anyone else at the table. If I do, I'll cry.

"Let's get going, then." Nono reaches a hand out to me. "I think your parents will be excited when they hear."

"Can't I call them on my own phone? And talk to my friend, to say why I can't make it on Saturday?" She has to let me do at least that.

But Nono's face says no. "Taking your phone away was punishment for lying to your grandfather and me, Cassie. I'm afraid that rule still holds. Those are the consequences of your behavior."

"But I—"

"Grandma Tess," Lana says at the same time, "it would only be two little texts. Can't Cassie just—"

"No," Nono says, firm. "End of discussion. Now let's get this adventure started! I promise it will be an experience to remember."

"The only thing I'm going to remember," I say, misery crowding my head and chest, "is that I wish I'd never come on this trip!"

"Cassie," Howie says, but I'm certainly not listening to *him* now. Instead I push myself out into the lobby, pounding on the elevator button. I can't believe Nono is doing this to me. Not only am I going to miss the most important event of the whole summer, but I can't even tell Kendra Mack why. And when Cory shows up, and I'm not there—

I run down the hall, desperate to get into our room. As soon as the door's shut behind me, I slide into a crumpled pile on the floor, lean my head on my knees, and finally let out the tears.

Chapter Twenty-Three

Lana

I feel truly terrible for Cassie, I do, but as soon as Nono said she wanted to catch the Magic Moment together, my heart lit up with the glow of a million fireflies and an ocean of phosphorescence. I'd love to see the place Grandpa Howe has told me so many stories about, and more than that, I know exactly what Grandma Tess meant when she said she bet at least one of us had a big wish to make. Catching the Magic Moment is the one thing I can do to save my mother. I can't pass it up.

After Cassie leaves in such a fit, Grandpa Howe stands and squeezes Grandma Tess around the shoulders before leading us to the elevator. "This is going to be a far better adventure," he says. "Cassie will come around."

I nod and follow, though I'm not sure, in Cassie's case, Grandpa Howe will be right.

I go to Grandma Tess and Grandpa Howe's room so we can all talk to my parents at the same time. Grandma Tess dials first and tells Mom what our plan is.

"I'm so glad we have your blessing, Frankie," she says to Mom. "Lana wants to say hi too."

I take the phone. "Hi, Mom."

When she says hi back, the worn-out sound of her voice makes my heart twist up. Now I'll be away from her even longer. It's to help make sure I don't lose her entirely, but suddenly I think that it might not be easy.

Her tiredness seems even bigger than yesterday. Like she's softer, blurrier. Maybe I should forget this plan and head straight home.

"Do you think I should go?" I ask her.

"Of course I think so, sweetie. Your father's burning with jealousy, but we're both excited for you. I think we can tough it out on our own for another week or two, even though we do miss you. I'm not up for much more than working and sleeping these days, anyhow. Having fun with your grandparents will be better than hanging around your weary old mom."

My throat clenches. Having fun with my grandparents

will be better than watching my mother die, she means. Maybe that's really how she'd prefer it—facing whatever this is without me there.

"How are you feeling right now?" I say.

"Oh," she says, more breath than voice, "for the most part okay. Frustrated that these headaches want to be a constant thing. I'm going to see Dr. Owen tomorrow in case she has suggestions, but it isn't anything to be worried about. I'm sure it's stress, mainly, which is always temporary. Please don't let it ruin your beautiful trip."

There are so many things she could be not saying, it makes my own head start to ache. "You sure you don't need me to come help?"

If she asked me to, I would. And then, I guess, at least Cassie would be happy.

"Oh no, honey. That's sweet of you, but we're really okay."

"I'll bring you back a rock from the beach," I say, since I still can't say all the other things.

"And spit in the ocean for me." She laughs.

We say "I love you" and hang up, and I head back to my room to pack. Even though Mom's glad we're going to Maine, if she's talking about actually going to the doctor now, I know it's continuing to get worse. We need to get to the Magic Moment, and we need to do it fast.

· · ·

When I let myself into our room, Cassie's sitting on her bed, clicking through channels with the TV remote instead of packing.

"Are you okay?" I ask.

"No, I'm not okay, but thank you for asking." Her voice is cold again, though at least this time I know why, and that the why isn't me.

"Do you want to talk about it?" I say.

She stares at the screen, channels flipping by so fast I can't tell what the shows are. I don't know what to do, exactly.

"I think Grandma Tess and Grandpa Howe are pretty keen on leaving soon."

"You all have a good time." She's still not looking at me. "I'm not going."

"Cassie, you can't stay here by yourself."

"I'm not staying here," she says. "I'm going to take the bus back. It's not that far, and I have money. I can get someone at the desk downstairs to help me."

Her chin is up and her voice is stiff, but both of us know no one will allow this to happen. Not even Grandpa Howe.

Before I can tell her so, there's a knock at our door.

"Cassie, I have your mother on the phone," Grandma Tess says from outside. "She'd like to speak with you, please."

Cassie rolls her eyes and unfolds herself, leaving the TV on some cooking show. She opens the door and glares at Grandma Tess, holding out her hand for the phone.

"I'm not going," Cassie says to her mom right away.

I head to the bedside table to collect my things. I think Grandma Tess should let Cassie talk to her mom in private, but she doesn't budge. I wonder if I should go into the bathroom and shut the door, so at least Cassie doesn't have to have this conversation in front of Grandma Tess *and* me.

There isn't much for us to overhear, though, because Cassie's mom is doing most of the talking. Cassie's end of the conversation sounds like: "No," and "Saturday," and "Yes," and "Kendra Mack." Then she listens for a while.

"Mom, I told you about it at, like, the beginning of summer. I told you about it before I left."

More listening. Cassie's mom obviously has a lot to say about this.

"But you let Tom go to his friends' almost every night." Cassie's voice climbs to a pitch that means she's fighting crying. "This is just one party."

There's another pause. I check my duffel, but only my pajamas need rerolling.

"No," she says, and then, "Yes, but—"

I do finally go into the bathroom, to get my toothbrush,

but mainly because I hate hearing how badly Cassie doesn't want to do this. The walls must be thin, or else Cassie's really loud, though, because I can't help hearing her groan, "How can they even drive that far? Besides, I have to start thinking about school." She waits, says, "No," a couple of times again, and finally, "Fine."

Grandma Tess says something to her that I can't make out. Cassie murmurs back, the door shuts, and there's the terrible sound of Cassie's sobs as she collapses on the bed again.

Though I'm not sure exactly what to do, I go sit next to her. Trying to rub her back like my mom does seems like it could be a good idea, or a bad one.

"It's so unfair," she says wetly. "Mom says she'll try to find Mrs. Mack's information in the PTA directory, since not showing up without sending word would be rude, but moms talking to other moms is what happens in *third grade*. It's worse than not telling Kendra Mack at all. At least then I could make up something really dramatic. And . . . just, *ugh* . . ." She cries harder.

"Cassie," I try, "I know it's terrible. I know it is. But maybe we can make it slightly less terrible. If you're on really, really good behavior, I bet Grandma Tess will give you your phone back as soon as tomorrow. Then you can still call everyone to explain, and I'm sure they'll understand.

They'll probably be more worried than mad."

"You don't know." She sits up to look at me. Her face is wet and messy, and strands of her straight black hair are sticking to her cheeks. I grab a bunch of tissues from the bathroom and hand them to her. She presses her face into the whole wad and cries some more.

"You have to help me keep this from happening," she says as soon as she can talk. "You have to, Lana. I can't not show up at this party. It'll be like death."

Cassie has no idea that if we don't go to Maine, it really *will* be like death, but I can't tell her that. She's upset right now, and I don't want to try and make this about me.

Still, every minute we sit here is a minute of lost fireflies. I have to get Cassie to stop crying and start packing. Once we get to the End of the Road, Cassie can wish for everything to be fine with her friends, and none of her worries will matter. So even though I'm breaking a rule that's so important between friends you don't even have to *say* it, I reach out, grip her shoulder, and lie.

"Cassie, I promise I will help you. But we need time to think up a truly good plan, and Grandma Tess is ready to go *now*. I think the best thing to do is put on a brave face, get in the car, and get on our way. We'll have plenty of time to plot from the backseat."

Her brows come together, and I think she'll start crying

again. "Okay," she says, like it's the most difficult thing she's ever been asked to do.

It's hard not to roll my eyes at the drama, but at least she's agreeing.

I get up from the bed and hold my hands out to her. She takes them, I pull, and we're one step closer to Maine.

Chapter Twenty-Four

Cassie

Eager as Nono is to drag me thousands of miles away from everything important, it's only about an hour into the drive before she asks Howie to look ahead to Sacramento and see if there are any good bookstores.

"We can grab some audiobooks if they have them," she says. "Or take turns reading out loud to each other. That might even be more fun."

I'm not reading a page of anything aloud, because I'm never speaking to Nono again. Lana and Howie are both totally on board, though, of course, and before long we're navigating to a small store called Time Tested Books. While everyone gets out, I stay put.

"I'm not interested," I tell Lana. She looks to Howie for help.

"Come on, Cassie." He leans in to give me a pat on the knee, but I move my legs away. "You'll be glad for the stretch a few hours from now."

"Let her do what she wants," Nono says, dismissing me and heading to the shop.

"Do you want me to get you anything?" Lana asks, lingering behind. Admittedly I'm curious if they have this series Cheyenne Taylor and Neftali Manji are obsessed with, but who cares, since they'll probably never talk to me again. Plus, if Nono isn't concerned whether or not I come inside, then I *really* don't want to go. Even though Lana's trying to be nice, I don't feel like being cheered up. I don't know if I'll ever be cheered up again.

"I have magazines in my bag. Those'll be fine," I say, crossing my arms over my chest.

She's disappointed, I can tell. As she walks away, I realize it might be fun to teach her Fiona's bookstore game of making up our own story or poem from titles on the shelves, but I don't want to be having fun right now. Especially not where Nono can see.

After what feels like forever, they come back to the car.

"Could've used you for a tiebreaker," Howie says,

handing me the bag of books. I look inside.

"*Little Women* was your Nono's suggestion, and Lana picked out *The Graveyard Book. Peter Pan*'s mine. That other one the bookseller recommended when she saw I had *Peter Pan.* We'll let you decide which one to read first."

"Definitely not *Little Women*," I say. I take the last one, *Tiger Lily*, from the bag and check out the description on the back. The story of a fierce warrior princess seems good, until I read she's part of a doomed romance. Far too close to my own misery right now.

Nono pretends I'm not ignoring her by ignoring me right back, and starts up the car. What she doesn't know is that I've had months of training from Kendra Mack. I can play this game much longer than she can.

Even with the book to distract us (*Peter Pan* is funny, and Howie does a good job of making it dramatic, though I don't admit I'm listening), the rugged mountain scenery, short yoga stretches every few hours, and a mini stop at some reservoir park in Nevada, it is still a long, long, *long* drive to Salt Lake City. We don't get to the hotel until almost ten thirty at night, and by the time we're checked in, we all want to go straight to bed.

I've had hours to brood on my plan to get us turned around in the morning, though, and this is the first chance

Lana and I have had to talk.

"A major illness won't work," I say before she's even put her duffel down.

"What?" she says, looking shocked.

"One of us faking sick. Too sick to keep going on this trip. It wouldn't work because we already tried that," I explain.

"Oh," she says. "Hang on and let me tell my parents we're here, okay?" She takes her time with it, the furrow between her brows getting deeper as she types. Obviously she's not rubbing it in my face that she has her phone and I don't, but it still feels that way, a little.

When she finishes, she plops down in the armchair by our window. "Well, we can't mess with the car. That would be dangerous, and also too hard to pull off."

I hadn't thought about doing anything to the car. That's brilliant.

"I read pouring sugar into the gas tank works," I say.

Lana frowns. "I'm pretty sure that would destroy it."

"So?" Nono's destroyed my life; I think her engine is a fair trade.

"So, wouldn't it be obvious who did it? And then wouldn't you be so grounded that even if we did go back home—which might be hard, with a broken car—there's no way your mom would let you go to any party?"

This is true. But I still like the car idea. If it means we're stranded here forever, at least Nono will miss out on that stupid Magic Moment, just like I'm missing out on Kendra Mack's.

"Isn't there, like, some doohickey under the car? A plug that holds in all the oil? We could crawl under there at one of our stops, unscrew it, and then the oil would pour out and the car wouldn't be able to go. Right? It'd be easy to fix, but I know my mom would think twice about letting me keep riding in a car that was so unpredictable."

Lana's not fully listening. She's gotten two chimes from her phone and is busy texting.

"What's up with that? You and your parents?" It's annoying how much she's been on the phone with them, especially when *I* need her attention.

Lana looks stricken. "What do you mean?"

"Nono and Howie are talking to them too, you know. You don't have to update them every ten seconds."

"It doesn't seem any different from you being on the phone with Kendra Mack all the time," she says. Her quick, disapproving tone surprises me.

"You don't have to get snitty about it. I'm just curious."

Lana makes a one-shouldered shrug. "We're close, is all. Don't you miss your parents? Your brother?"

It hadn't occurred to me before, but I'm actually glad to

be on a bit of a vacation from my family. Especially Tom and his unrelenting perfectness. It's been nice to have a week when I don't have to worry about being compared to him.

"Honestly? No," I say.

Lana lifts her chin. "Well, I guess we're just different, then."

She seems just as annoyed with me as I was with her a second ago. Maybe it should make me madder, but I'm impressed she's not being a pushover. Her not backing down also makes me notice how rude I just sounded. I wonder how Izzy Gathing would act if someone did the same thing to her.

"So, back to the car thing." I change the subject.

"I don't know." Lana rolls her head against the back of the chair. "What if we broke down in the middle of the highway? That could be really dangerous. And when would we do it? It's not like we're getting that much time to ourselves."

"Okay, what, then?" I sink down to the floor at her feet. "We have to think of something, and we have to do it fast, or we'll have gone too far to get back in time."

"We're already pretty far."

"I know! That's why we have to think!"

Lana shakes her head. "What I think is we're both tired.

It's been a long day, and our brains are foggy. I think the main thing we need now is some sleep."

"Okay, but Rule Number Eleven is We Will Definitely Talk About It in the Morning."

Lana sticks out her hand to shake, but her phone beeps again. When she checks it, she looks relieved.

"Your parents again?" The tiniest scrap of an idea is glimmering in my mind.

"Just saying good night."

"You miss them, don't you?" I push. The idea glows brighter.

"I told you I did," she says.

I suck in a breath to calm how excited I suddenly feel. "Miss them so bad it'd be terrible to be away from them for another week, right? And we might be gone even longer."

The expression on her face is one I can't decipher. "Well, not if—"

"So, tomorrow at breakfast, we go down and explain to Howie and Nono that after sleeping on it for a night, you've decided you're just too homesick to keep going. They know how close you are to your parents. They'll totally understand."

"Cassie, there's a reason—"

I kneel in front of her, clasping my hands together. "Lana, please. I'm begging you. You know how important it is, and this plan is the only one that will work. Howie adores you, and so does Nono. They'll do anything you ask them. Please, Lana, you have to. We can go to Maine with them any other summer. Just not right now. Please? Please say you'll do this for me."

"Well—" She chews on her lip and looks down at the phone still in her hand. "It would be good to be back with them."

I wrap my arms around her knees and squeeze them tight. "Thank you. From the bottom of my heart a million times, thank you. I will make this up to you one day, I swear. We should make a rule about it."

She nudges me away with her foot and stands up. "We don't have to do that."

We brush our teeth and get into our pajamas. When Lana turns out the light between our beds, I lie there awhile seeing visions in the dark: Nono's car doing a complete U-turn. Arriving back in my own driveway. Getting out my outfit for Kendra Mack's party. And best of all, walking out to her patio, straight over to say hi to Cory Baxter.

Chapter Twenty-Five

Lana

I was so distracted by Cassie's idea last night that I forgot to set my alarm. Forgot, too, that Cassie doesn't have her phone, so the only thing that wakes us is Grandma Tess calling to say it's almost time to leave.

"I'll shower quick, I promise!" Cassie says as she bounces out of bed.

"Yeah, right."

She makes a face and tosses a pillow at me, but at least she's in a better mood. The cloud of yuckiness she was in yesterday would be hard to take for another eleven-hour drive, though maybe today it'll be my turn to be in a funk. I promised Cassie I'd help her, but I need to get to Maine to make that wish.

While Cassie's in the shower, I call Mom to see if she's feeling better like she was last night. When she doesn't pick up, I leave a quick "good morning" message and try Dad. Maybe Mom's still sleeping if she's not feeling well, but I know Dad will be up, since morning temperatures are better for working outside.

But he doesn't answer, either.

I leave another quick voice mail, trying not to listen to the alarm bells ringing in my head, and pace around the room, trying to remember every stop-worrying tip that Tamika's ever told me, like "Stress only comes from resisting what is actually happening." But that one doesn't help in this case. It's not like Mom or Dad to not pick up the phone when I call. Even when they're meeting with clients, they answer to make sure there isn't an emergency and tell me they'll call back.

As backup, I text Mom **Hi and good morning from Utah**, and when Cassie comes out of the bathroom, I take my phone in with me. Cassie's made fun of me for talking to my parents so much, but I have a terrible feeling she'll finally understand why I do before too much longer. Telling her now is out of the question. I know she doesn't believe in the Magic Moment, so if she knew what was wrong with Mom, she'd use it as even more of a reason to get us turned around, instead of hearing me out about getting east. Maybe that wouldn't be true, but I'm not sure I want to find out.

No messages come in while I'm brushing my teeth and pulling my hair into a quick ponytail. As I get dressed, one of Tamika's favorite Eleanor Roosevelt quotes pops into my head: *You must do the thing you think you cannot do.* But I can't make myself stop being scared.

Maybe Mom's already dead. Maybe Dad's so wrapped in his own devastation that he hasn't figured out how to tell me yet. Maybe yesterday was the last time I will ever talk to her. Maybe she'll never hear the voice mail I just left.

"Maybe during breakfast is when you should do it," Cassie says as I step out of the bathroom.

A sound like *huh?* comes out of me.

Cassie makes big, exasperated eyes. "Talk to Howie. I can pull Nono away to apologize or something. Then you can ask him to go home. What do you think?"

"Oh." What I think is I want to hear back from my parents. "I'm not sure that's going to be the right moment. Maybe I should wait for him to have a full, happy stomach."

There are three bright knocks on our door, and Grandma Tess calls out, "Morning, girls! Time to hit the road!"

Cassie looks at me in panic, but I can't help feeling relieved.

"Coming!" I call through the door.

"When, then?" Cassie whispers, fierce. She's turned mean in a too-familiar way.

"When the time is right," I tell her, too worried and tired of this to sass back.

Grandma Tess wants to look at Great Salt Lake before we head out of town, but since we don't have time to actually swim in it, it isn't that fun. As soon as we get there, Cassie takes Grandma Tess's hand and asks if they can walk along the shore a ways, lifting her eyebrows pointedly at me. For a second Grandpa Howe looks like he's up for a stroll, but Grandma Tess shields her eyes with her hand, gazes across the flat water, and says, "I just wanted to see it. Now I have, and we should get going."

I take a few pictures of the salt incrustations along the banks to send my dad. Tamika would be interested in the amazing facts Grandpa Howe reads to us about how the Native Americans collected salt here for curing meat. Dad, I hope, will just find them interesting and strange. And a reason to finally text back.

But he doesn't. Through the rest of Utah and across the border into Wyoming, Cassie and I pass her notebook back and forth, playing Hangman. We're both tense, but I make Cassie laugh a few times with the googly-eyed faces I draw.

The game takes my mind off my parents, but not much.

As we're heading into the first city in Wyoming, Cassie writes in the margin of her notebook, *You need to talk to him at this stop*, and I think she's right, I do—I need to tell Grandpa Howe that I haven't heard from my parents all day and I'm worried. I need to tell him he has to fill me in on what's really going on. But before I answer Cassie, Grandpa Howe's phone starts ringing. He checks the screen and says, "It's Peter," to Grandma Tess. She probably doesn't mean to, but I see her glance with concern in the rearview mirror back at me.

"Hi, son," Grandpa Howe answers.

Cassie pushes the notebook into my lap, wanting me to write back or at least guess a letter, but suddenly I can't see anything on the paper. Instead there are whirling pinwheels of pink-and-yellow panic around my eyes, and my heartbeat is thrumming in my ears.

But I hear Grandpa Howe perfectly when he asks, "How is she feeling now?"

Grandma Tess takes the very next exit and pulls over in the parking lot of a gas station.

"Come on, girls. Let's take a pit stop. I could use some more water, and I'm sure your grandfather thinks eleven thirty in the morning is the perfect time for a Snickers break."

I don't want to go even a foot farther away from news of my mom, but I need to prepare myself for whatever it is Dad's telling Grandpa Howe. I follow Grandma Tess and Cassie into the gas station bathroom, lock my stall door, and sit straight down on the toilet. My mom is dying, I know it. Or she's already dead. It was a panicky thought this morning, but now it really might be true. I try to say it in my head over and over, to get some tears out now, so that when I hear my dad or Grandpa Howe say the actual words to me maybe I won't cry as hard, but all I feel is hollow and dry.

Grandma Tess knows something terrible is happening too, because when we're all finished in the bathroom, she tells Cassie to come along instead of lingering in the chip aisle. I don't even glance at the candy. I can see Grandpa Howe is still on the phone with Dad, but he's out of the car and leaning against the hood. When I push open the door, I leave a sweaty palm print on the glass, even though my body's gone cold.

"She's here," Grandpa Howe says when I get to him. He gives Grandma Tess a sad smile, puts a hand on my shoulder, and walks me away from the car before handing me the phone.

"Dad?" I watch Grandma Tess and Cassie head across the parking lot and off on a little walk, to give me some privacy. So the news must really be awful.

"Hi, Lanalee. How are you doing?" Dad's voice is sad and scared, and trying not to be either of those things. Hearing it kicks me into some kind of strong-girl gear I didn't know I had.

"What's wrong with Mom?" I say, wishing I'd been brave enough to ask it weeks ago.

"Straight shooter, that's good," Dad says. "You're right. It's how I should be, too."

He tells me, calm as he can, that in the middle of the night Mom's headache got so bad she was throwing up. That he wrapped her in a blanket, carried her to the car, and brought her to the hospital. While I listen, I picture how strong Dad needed to be to do that. I know I need to be that strong for him, no matter what else I'm feeling.

He goes on. "This morning when you called we were with the doctor, getting some scans. We're still waiting for the results, but they've given Mom some good medicine to help with the pain."

"When are they going to know anything?" I can't believe how grown-up I sound, but it seems to help Dad not freak out, which helps me not freak out, either. At least, not as much.

"It may be any minute, may be another few hours. It's hard to tell around here. I wanted to get as much information as possible before I called. When I got your awesome pictures, though, it felt wrong to have you so far away and not knowing. Tell me what you're thinking. What do you need?"

I stare across the road. *I need to get to the End of the Road*, is all I can think. I look up at Grandpa Howe, who's been standing next to me with his arm draped across my back the whole time. Beyond him I can see the small, white-and-blue blobs that are Grandma Tess and Cassie heading back toward us on the shoulder of the road. This minute is when I could do what Cassie wants and ask to come home, and then I would be there to help my parents through whatever this turns out to be. But depending on what Mom's scans say, catching the Magic Moment might be more important than ever.

"Can I think about it?" I ask both Grandpa Howe and Dad at the same time.

Grandpa Howe nods, once. Dad says, "Of course."

We're quiet a minute before Dad says, "I'll call you as soon as we've talked to the doctors. We want you to try not to worry too much and keep having fun, but if you decide you want to turn around and come home, nobody has any trouble with that—we've already discussed it with your grandparents. But Mom and I will be glad for you if you decide to keep going and get to see the End of the Road."

My throat trembles, thinking this whole time they've been talking about me, but not to me. So that my dad doesn't have to hear me cry, on top of all the terrible he must already feel, I quickly tell him to kiss Mom for me and get a kiss back, and we hang up.

Grandpa Howe hands me his handkerchief, but I don't need it. Yet. I keep watching Cassie and Grandma Tess getting closer and closer. I have no idea how to tell Cassie any of this, or whether I should.

Beside me, Grandpa Howe waits. Finally he says, "Is this something you want to discuss, all four of us together?"

I look up at him, wondering how my grandfather got to be so smart about what's happening inside people's minds. I shake my head, telling him no.

Once Cassie finds out any of this, she'll know I could easily get us back home. But Grandpa Howe seems to feel as I do that the best place for me now is the End of the Road. We both know without saying that Mom could use a little magic.

Chapter Twenty-Six

Cassie

I don't know what Howie and Lana talked about during her perfect opportunity to get us headed back, but it's clear that abandoning this End of the Road business wasn't it. When Nono and I get back from "stretching our legs and getting some air," neither Lana nor Howie says a word about whatever Lana and her dad needed to discuss privately. Howie takes his turn behind the wheel, and Lana asks Nono if she'll read more from *Peter Pan*. I hand her my notebook with a big question mark drawn on it, but she shakes her head. I push it farther in her lap, insisting she at least explain what her dad said, but she only writes *I need to rest for a little bit*.

Which, okay. Maybe the phone call made it necessary

for this to be done in two parts, and she's biding her time. Lana's smart, and I trust her. I can wait. So long as we're turned around by lunch.

When we stop for a bathroom break in Rock Springs— which really should just be called *Rock*—I expect *this* will be the moment, but Lana simply trades seats with me and asks if *she* can have a turn reading. For the first time, it seems like she's shutting me out. It's as nauseating and uncomfortable as when Kendra Mack was reading Fiona's diary. A bad, unsettled feeling suggests there's more going on in my friend's head than I know. Once I find out, I may not like it.

I stare out the window, but there's nothing to look at. I'm getting even more antsy. I ask Nono if I can use her phone, to find us a place to eat, but Nono's Don't-Let-Cassie-Near-a-Gadget thing is holding strong. "I think your grandfather's done a grand job of finding places for us so far," she says. "Let's see what he can come up with next."

He's not my grandfather, I grumble in my head, but I know better than to say it. Howie tells me it's still another hour and a half before the next stop, anyway. I take out one of the magazines I brought, but after about twenty pages of flipping, almost all I can think about is my friends, and the party, and all the fun I'll miss, if Lana doesn't say something fast.

By the time we get to Rawlins, I'm about to crawl out of my skin. Since Lana stopped reading a while ago, we've been listening to Nono's playlist again. It's cycling through a croony phase that makes me want to turn the car around just to escape this terrible music.

The restaurant for our late lunch is small and ugly on the outside, but at least inside there's a gift shop and some delicious smells pouring from the kitchen. My stomach growls. As we wait for a table, I go over to the postcards and spin the rack as hard as I can, which is when I hear Howie's phone ring behind me.

I'm tired of being in the dark. Something's going on that's ruining my life, and it's time I knew what. I duck down on the other side of the rack so Howie can't see me, but I can still listen.

He says, "Okay," a lot. Then, "When do they want to schedule it?" He heads toward Nono and Lana.

I follow behind as casually as I can, stopping to pretend I'm interested in some tacky T-shirts with a bunch of horseshoes on them. Howie hands Lana the phone, which is right when the hostess calls for us.

Nono gives me a tense smile. "How about we sit down and let Lana finish her conversation?"

I go only because I have to. But Howie stays behind in the gift shop with Lana, and suddenly I'm glad we got separated. When she hangs up with her dad, she'll have a moment alone to finally talk to Howie about her homesickness.

Nono and I get seated. She picks up her menu and says, "Cassandra, let's just try to focus on our lunch, okay? I think I could eat five of these tacos."

I'm hungry too, but my curiosity is much bigger. I keep one eye on the menu and one eye on Lana, whose face has turned white. I can't take any more of this.

"I'm going to go wash my hands." I stand up and head for the restroom without waiting for Nono's answer, but instead of going in, I loop back over to the rack of ugly T-shirts. From there I have a good view of Howie and Lana, and better than that—I can hear them.

"If you need us to head back," Howie says, "even with what you told your dad, we can do that right now. Tess and I both want whatever you want, Pumpkin."

I can't believe it. Here it is—the moment when Lana saves the day. I don't know how she managed to orchestrate it so perfectly, but I can't wait to hug her.

She looks up at him, still pale, but also determined.

"What I want," she says, "is to catch the Magic Moment."

I'm paralyzed with shock. Not even my heart is beating in my chest. Howie just offered to take us home—to turn the car around *right this minute*—and she *isn't* going to do it? I'm not sure I can breathe. I didn't think anyone could be more two-faced than Fiona.

I stay frozen behind the T-shirts as Howie pats Lana on the back and says, "That's what we'll do, then." He heads for the table, and Lana goes toward the restrooms.

Before I can think, I'm stomping across the store. I shove the bathroom door open so hard, it slams against the wall behind it and bounces back. Lana's standing at the sink, pressing wet paper towels to her face. The noise of my barging in makes her jump.

"Lana Thorton-Howe, you're going to tell me why you just betrayed me, and you're going to tell me right now. We had the perfect plan to end this trip, but when you got your chance—a real, obviously important chance—you said no." I cross my arms and lean against the bathroom door to stop myself from attacking her. "Rule Number Twelve is Tell Me the Truth, and Do It *Now*. I'm not letting you leave this bathroom until you do."

She looks at me and takes in a shaky breath. The bottom ridges of her eyes start to glimmer. She's been so stone-cold and quiet all morning, it surprises me. But I will not feel sorry for her. I won't.

"Cassie," she says, wiping her eyes, "I really don't want to let you down—I really don't. But I can't turn back now."

She's so upset, I feel an urge to try and stop her tears. I

want to stay mad, but the way her voice is shaking has got me worried. I take a few steps toward her. "What is it?"

She looks at the floor, but I can see her face close off as she shuts down the emotions and shuts me out. "I don't think I—"

Something inside me snaps. It feels like Kendra Mack and Izzy Gathing with their secrets. Like the way Tom laughs with his friends but says, "Nothing," when I ask what's so funny, or how this whole week not even my own grandmother is on my side. It's like Fiona keeping her real thoughts about me in her diary, instead of trusting me with the truth. That Lana's doing it too is way too much.

"You're so selfish!" I holler. "You say no one talks to you, but you never tell anybody anything about yourself. It's not only hotel rooms you don't know how to share. No wonder you don't have any real friends!"

I storm out. There's nowhere for me to go besides back to the table, but I don't want to sit there with her. I don't want to be anywhere near her for one more minute, let alone the rest of this trip. I thought Lana was my friend, but now she's intentionally ruining my whole life, and she won't even tell me why.

"I'm not hungry," I tell Nono and Howie when I get back to the table. "May I please, please go back to the car and wait for you there?"

"Don't be silly." Nono pulls out the chair next to her. "We're all starving. Have some chips and salsa, at least. What's gotten into you? You're flushed. Sit down and have some water."

"I don't—" I start, but Lana's coming over.

"Cinnamon churros with chocolate dipping sauce first sound good to you?" Howie says, squeezing her shoulder as she sits down.

She looks at me, but I pull my eyes away quick. If she's not going to tell me why she's abandoning me right now, at this most crucial point, then I'm not telling her anything, ever. Not even with my eyes.

Chapter Twenty-Seven

Lana

No wonder you don't have any real friends, Cassie's voice repeats in my head. I was already reeling from what Dad had told me about Mom, but this almost hurts more, because it's right here, instead of states away. Of all the people in the world I'd never want to hurt, Cassie is at the top. I know she deserves an explanation, but by the time I'd recovered from my shock, she was already sitting with Grandma Tess and Grandpa Howe, acting like nothing in the world had happened.

All through lunch, she won't look at me. When I try to say anything, even "Grandma Tess, could you hand me another napkin?" she talks over me like I'm not there, asking Grandpa Howe silly things like are there any snakes at the End of the Road, and is there even a working toilet. She's trying to make me feel bad, I can tell. Trying to say, through her questions about how long it would take an ambulance to get out there if someone got hurt, that she can't think of a more awful place to have to go. And that it's all my fault for forcing her.

At first it makes me sad, but when we're walking back to the car and she still ignores me, even though I know she hears me call her name, it starts to make me angry. Cassie said I was selfish, but a big reason why I haven't said anything yet to her about my mom is because we've been so focused on all *her* dramas. Now, when I've just found out that there is actually a tumor on Mom's brain—that she'll have to have surgery to find out if it's cancerous—and these headaches are truly life-threatening, Cassie acts like even making eye contact with me will give her a disease.

It makes the next eight hours to Omaha, Nebraska, absolutely awful. Besides the tension between Cassie and me inside the car—and all the terrible thoughts and sadness about my mom and her brain and hospitals and my poor dad—outside of it, everything is dry and dusty, and there's nothing interesting to look at except for flat, flat, flat. Even Grandma Tess's music is either sad or angry sounding. The only thing that helps me endure it is knowing that every mile gets us closer to the Magic Moment, where I can wish all of this away. Even Dad said he thought it would help.

After our twelve-hour drive, Grandpa Howe and Grandma Tess find out there's karaoke in the lounge at our hotel and decide to sing a few rounds. I understand it's probably to help take their minds off Mom, but there's no way I'm singing. Being stuck in a room with Cassie enduring more of her silent treatment doesn't sound good either, but I can't think of another place to go. She obviously feels the same way, since the minute the door shuts behind us she locks herself in the bathroom and starts filling the tub. It feels extra mean of her to run a bath for herself when she can tell I'm upset, plus I'm the one who told her baths could help you feel better. As tears tremble at the edges of my eyes, I try to channel some of Tamika's bravery and decide to crawl into bed to start her a letter. Even after only a few lines, telling her what's happening feels better and reminds me I *do* have real friends. Even if Cassie's never going to be one of them.

The next morning, our grandparents call our room at 7:17. When Cassie gets off the phone with Grandma Tess, she turns her back and pretends to look for something in her suitcase.

Which, fine—I hope she knows I don't want to talk to

her, either. I've been making all the overtures so far this trip, and I'm not doing that again. I have other things to worry about than Cassie.

I realize we're in a different time zone now, and that what's early in the morning for us is super early for Mom and Dad, so I don't send a message first thing, because I want Mom to be getting her sleep, though it's hard not to. When she finally texts on our way to Chicago, relief washes over me.

Well, it's official. Dad's cooking is way better than hospital food.

I smile and hold up the phone so Grandma Tess can see.

Tell the nurses about Dessert First, I tell her. **At least the pudding should be all right.**

I'm glad my mom is joking, but still it feels like Dad's trick—to laugh off bad subjects.

How are you? I ask.

Tired of waiting. Ready to be home, and to have the surgery scheduled. These doctors take forever. What about you?

I pause, unsure how I really am.

"Gee, Lana," Cassie's fake-sweet voice breaks in. "You sure are on your phone a lot lately. Why, it seems like you're not really here with us."

Before I can even process what a mean thing that was

to say, or how to snap back at her, Grandma Tess reaches behind the seat, grips Cassie's knee in her hand, and says, "That's enough." To keep from looking at either of them, I type back to Mom that I'm ready for her to be home too, and ready for us to get to Maine. While I'm sliding my phone back in my pocket, I catch Cassie's eye by accident, and for a second she looks almost apologetic, but then she just snottily raises her chin.

Maybe, I think, the reason Cassie gets along with Kendra Mack and her awful friends so well is because she actually deserves them.

When we arrive in Chicago late-late that afternoon, Grandpa Howe is energized by being in a big, bustling city, and I'm grateful for his determination to keep this fun. He makes sure to get us a glossy hotel right on what he calls the Magnificent Mile, and before we even get into the elevator to put our bags in our room, he's already talking to a lady at a desk about what we should see first.

"How about a stroll over to Millennium Park?" he asks us when she's done with her recommendations. "You girls have got to see the Bean."

I have no idea what this is, and I can feel Cassie wondering as much as I am, but when our eyes connect, we look away.

"You do; it's beautiful," Grandma Tess says. "And then we'll have gotten plenty of exercise and can go for a nice, big steak dinner."

"Sounds like good thinking to me." Grandpa Howe puts an arm around Grandma Tess. Cassie hooks her arm in Grandma Tess's other one, so I purposely move over to the opposite side, putting our grandparents in the middle.

Grandma Tess and Grandpa Howe trade Chicago stories while we walk, seeming surprised when they find they'd both visited the same places at different times, and excited to tell each other about the spots they'd each been to that the other hadn't. Their happy storytelling is nice, but all I can think of is how whatever I see today I'll never get to share with my mom if they find out she really has cancer and she dies like Nana Lilia did. The Magic Moment could fix all that, I guess, but what if—even after we get there, after all of this—I'm still not able to catch it? Then Mom and Dad will never be old together the way my grandparents are.

I try to use Dad's "interested eyes" again when we reach Millennium Park, but it's hard to make it fun. People are everywhere—some spread out on blankets in whatever grass there is—enjoying the day. Two boys on skateboards take turns showing off tricks, and when one of them zooms in front of us, I can't help wondering if Cassie thinks he might be cute. Not that I care what she thinks anymore. The Bean itself is a huge, glossy silver bean standing as tall as a building in the middle of a courtyard, with plenty of space for people to walk under it and take pictures in the mirrored surface. Grandpa Howe asks a woman nearby if she'll take our picture, so we pose, Cassie and I staying on opposite sides. I know our grandparents can see that we can hardly stand to be around each other, which makes me feel worse about everything, if that's possible. I was so determined not to ruin this trip for them. Maybe this was a mistake. Maybe we should just go home.

I decide to call Mom again. If she wants me there for her surgery, I'll give up this Maine fantasy and go where I'm needed.

Standing away from the Bean, but still within Grandpa Howe's sight, I wait two rings, three, before she picks up.

"Hey there, Freckles."

I smile at the sound of her voice. "Hi, Mom. How are you feeling?"

"Better," she says, sounding it at least a little. "We've got the surgery scheduled for Tuesday. The doctors just left and I was about to text you, so your timing is great. Where are you now? Chicago, Dad said?"

I tell her about our city walk and the park we're in. She tells me she'd love to see it, and maybe we'll go together next summer. I swallow hard. Maybe it won't be that bad, if Mom's talking about trips. But then I remember Grandpa Howe and Nana Lilia thought they'd be taking trips too.

"I wish you were here now instead of in the hospital," I say. "Tell me about the surgery."

She explains that the tumor is located on the left side of her brain, just between her temple and her ear, where it's easy to reach, which is good. She says they'll have to shave half her head, but that Dad thinks that will make her look more punk. The procedure will take a long time—several hours—and she may have to be in the hospital awhile after.

What she's not saying is that in order to get to the tumor, they're going to have to slice open her skull with a little circular saw. I've seen it on TV, when Tamika was in her brain surgeon mode and couldn't get enough of those medical shows. Mom's also not saying that when they take it out, maybe they'll accidentally get some of her healthy brain, too, and she'll lose her vision, or her leg muscles, or even her memory. Or that even if that doesn't happen, she'll still have to go through a lot of rehab afterward. The worst part, of course—that it could be cancer, and that could mean it's also spread—neither one of us wants to mention.

"They're sending me home before too much longer," she finishes. "The pain's been managed, and I've had about every test you can think of. All we have to do is wait."

"Do you need me there?" I finally brave.

"This isn't like being sick in a way where you need a lot of help," Mom says. "I would hate for you to miss seeing the End of the Road just to sit around here. I want you to keep having fun adventures, so you'll have lots of stories to tell me while I'm recovering."

"Okay," I say, not sure whether to press. I do want to make the Magic Moment, but suddenly hearing that Mom doesn't need me at home makes me want to be there. Telling her that I want to curl up in her lap, so she can stroke my hair and make me feel better, when *she's* still in the hospital, feels like what Cassie called me in the bathroom yesterday—selfish.

"I love you, Mom," I say instead.

She tells me she loves me too, and not to worry, she'll soon be safe at home. Tears prick in my eyes at the thought of that, but when we hang up, I know the only thing left for me to do is make that wish.

Chapter Twenty-Eight

Cassie

When Lana slips away from that stupid Bean, I decide to follow her. She's easy to find in the crowd, thanks to her patchwork cap. There are people all around, so it's not hard to mix in, though I keep expecting her to look up and see me. But she's so oblivious, I'm able to stand almost right behind her, hearing every word she says. The whole time I'm listening, part of me *wants* her to see me, but when she hangs up, she heads back without even looking around.

For a minute I just stand there, stunned by what she's said. I should feel bad, but instead I'm even angrier than before. Lana's mother is in the hospital, but she's said nothing? It's ninety times worse than anything Fiona never told me about. And Nono didn't tell me either, for that matter, though she's been more than happy to spill to Lana all kinds of details about me and my life. That they'd keep that kind of secret, and act like *I'm* the bad guy, is just too awful to stand. I want Lana's mother to be okay, but also I want this stupid trip to be *over*.

On the way back to the hotel, Nono has to tell me to stop and slow down three times, I'm walking so fast. When we finally get to the lobby, she says, "I think Cassie and I need a minute."

Of course she never needs a minute with *Lana*, whose back I glare at as she and Howie head to the elevators.

"Cassie, this behavior has got to stop." Nono sinks onto the nearest couch. "You've been cold and distant, barely talking to me, and you and Lana aren't speaking at all—"

"Right, *I'm* the one who isn't talking," I say as meanly as I can.

Her neck straightens, and she pulls her head back. "What do you mean?"

I cross my arms. "You wanted me to be here with you and for us to share things, but you've been keeping this secret from me about Lana's mother the whole time. You won't let me talk to my friends, but you won't talk to me about things, either!"

Instead of being angry at me for talking back, Nono looks surprised.

"I didn't tell you about Frankie's brain tumor, darling, because for one thing, we didn't know for sure what it was until yesterday. Secondly, this hasn't been my story to tell. If Lana's kept that from you, perhaps she's had her reasons."

A funny feeling shimmers in the back of my head, Nono talking about it not being her story to tell, but mostly I'm shocked by the words *brain tumor*. If that's how bad it is, then Lana really isn't my friend. I can't imagine any reason you wouldn't want to talk about such a thing right away.

"Maybe we haven't done this right." Nono sighs again. "Come on."

She stands up and leads me down a hall. Before I know it we're back at Nono's car and she's unlocking the glove compartment.

"Here," she says, stretching out her hand. Lying flat in her palm is my phone. "Talking to people is important." Her face is apologetic. "I wanted you here, talking with us, but if I say I don't want to keep things from you, which is true, there's no sense in me keeping this from you, too. I hope you'll be respectful about it, but if there are people you need to be talking to, you should."

I don't know what to say. This is everything I wanted, but it also somehow isn't what I want at all.

"We need to go get ready for dinner," Nono says. "Howie's been looking forward to Morton's since Omaha."

I nod, but food is the last thing on my mind.

After being in Nono's car for so long, my phone battery is completely dead. I have to wait until it's charged overnight before I can even turn it on, which is torture. When Lana's alarm goes off in the morning, she checks to see if I'm awake but doesn't say anything. I don't say anything to her, either. Today is Saturday, the day of Kendra Mack's pool party. The day I was supposed to be back. Now we're up early, because Howie and Nono want to get as close to Maine as possible, which still isn't going to be close enough.

In the bathroom, I turn on the shower, but I don't get in right away. Instead I press my phone on and wait. I'm just as nervous as I was at the amusement park, but I can't count on Lana to help me this time.

There are several texts, most of them from the day Nono took my phone, plus a missed call from Kendra Mack. I decide to listen to her voice mail first.

"Hey, Cassie Parker!" Her voice is friendly and bright. "I hope you're okay. None of us have been able to get in touch with you. Hope everything's fabulous with you and

Cory"—she singsongs his name, and I can hear Izzy Gathing's nostril-breathing giggles in the background—"and you haven't, like, dropped off the planet or anything. It would be awful if you weren't at my party." There's more muffled laughter. "So, gimme a call when you get this message, m'kay? Dying to hear from you."

I desperately scroll through my texts, a panicky feeling creeping up my spine. Two new texts from Cory: **You wanna go out sometime?** which, yes, but then: **Cassie baby, don't leave me hanging,** which is even dumber than the ones he sent before. There's a text from Kendra Mack asking am I okay, and another one on its heels from Izzy Gathing, saying Cory Baxter wants to know if my mommy won't let me go on a date with him. That's apparently when Kendra Mack decided to call.

The last text is from Kendra Mack, sent the day before yesterday: **My mom told me you can't come on Saturday. Too bad. Have fun in Maine!** It's impossible to tell whether she's being snarky or nice.

Hands shaking, I hit reply, trying to figure out not only what to say, but also how to feel. Part of me wants to cry, looking at all of Cory's texts. No longer blinded by my first thrill, it's clear to me now that no real boy would write texts like these, especially not someone like Cory. I know this was all a big joke. Which makes another part of me furious that Kendra Mack would do this to me. Mostly, though, I'm horrified. The idea of them laughing at me this whole time makes me feel so sick I have to sit down on the edge of the tub. I even sent them that embarrassing selfie. Who knows who else has seen these texts by now, or who else knows about my crush. I am utterly, wholly, and completely mortified.

There's nothing for me to do but get in the shower.

While I'm rinsing the second round of conditioner out of my hair, a thing that Kendra Mack once said when Neftali Manji had one of her freak-outs comes to me: *Act like everything's fine and it will be fine*. Maybe Nono taking away my phone was the best thing that could have happened. By not responding to them at all, maybe I've shown that I'm above this. Maybe enough time has passed and everything's blown over. Probably by now they've got five other jokes going on. If I act cool, I can still save face, and still have a life back home. Just because they made fun of me for a minute doesn't mean my friends hate me. They make fun of each other all the time.

As I sugar-scrub my elbows and feet, I compose what I'll say: that my phone went haywire and I'm only just now getting their messages. Then, something like, *You really thought I'd fallen for that Cory Baxter thing? Ha, right. Joke's on you*.

I mouth the words under the streaming water, holding my hand to my chest like I'm being haughty. It doesn't feel good, but if it's what I have to do to keep from being mocked and, worse, ostracized, then I will. It might even give them all something to talk about at the party today— *Oh, that Cassie's so funny. It's not the same without her here.* Them wishing I were there is certainly much, much better than being glad that I'm not.

When I get out, I wipe the steam off the mirror with the edge of my towel. I have to practice looking aloof four times before I hit on the right expression, and then I do it over to make sure it sticks. What's happened is awful, but I've survived worse—this isn't near as bad as when Fiona vanished from my life forever—and I certainly won't be letting on to Lana about any of it now.

Chapter Twenty-Nine

Lana

Cassie has her precious phone back. I don't realize it until after breakfast, when we're already on the road and she asks Grandma Tess if it's okay to text her parents. That explains why she took even longer in the bathroom than usual—she had to get straight back to her friends. I lean forward and ask Grandpa Howe to pick the next playlist for us, turning my back to her. I don't care what her friends have been saying.

Thanks to more singing good songs and some new stories from Grandpa Howe and Grandma Tess, plus a few <3 texts from my mom, I'm almost even able to forget about Cassie. We stop in Cleveland for a decent lunch and a short walk, but then it's back in the car. Grandma Tess and

Grandpa Howe swap driving every few hours, and we start reading *Tiger Lily*, which is nowhere near as entertaining as *Peter Pan* or *The Graveyard Book*. I'm not paying super-close attention anyway, since all I want to hear is that my mom is back safe at home. Still, I don't want to text too much and bother them.

We're almost to our stop for the night in Schenectady when my parents finally call. It's a short conversation, since they're both very tired. Dad says home certainly is a better place to wait than the hospital, and I almost say, *Or a thousand miles away*, but then I remember this is how they want it. Even with a brain tumor, Mom doesn't really need me. Except to stay out of her way.

Though their call is what I've been waiting for all day, my heart still feels heavy and sad when we hang up. It makes me realize that even though Cassie has her phone back, and today is the Big Day of Kendra Mack's Pool Party, things have stayed quiet on her side of the car, too. I heard it buzz, once, sometime in the middle of the morning, but when I took a quick glance, I could see it was just her brother. If I weren't trying to de-friend her in my mind, I'd be a little concerned. It seems like all Cassie cares about is her group back home, but from their silence today, I wonder if they still care about her.

Too bad she decided to yell and turn her back on me

two days ago, because I might have been the only person she had left. I hope she regrets it and realizes that now.

As soon as we drop our bags in the hotel closet, Cassie flops on her bed and turns on the TV. In the bathroom, I change into my pajamas and brush my teeth. I'm not ready to go to sleep, but I'm not in the mood for any more reading, and I don't want to finish Tamika's letter until after Mom's surgery, either. I've already said good night to my parents, so texting them again is silly, and Grandpa Howe and Grandma Tess definitely need their sleep. Maybe Cassie's the only person I have right now, too. Which I guess means I'll just stare at the TV for a while, because I'm certainly not talking to *her*.

I haven't forgotten what she said, though, about people not talking to me because I don't talk to them, either.

When I come back out of the bathroom, she's still watching TV.

"All yours," I say, to say something.

She gets up from the bed as huffily as she can, takes her pajamas and toiletry bags from her suitcase, and disappears behind the door.

The truth is, I don't know how to act in a fight like this. We've created so many rules on this trip, and none of them are any help. Tamika and I have never fought, except the one time ages ago when I was too scared to try jumping backward across a deep ditch on our obstacle course, and she got annoyed that it ruined her game. But when that happened, I just biked home early, and the next day she called to see if I wanted to test out her new ice cream sundae experiment. We didn't talk about it—we just got over it.

Maybe it can be that simple for me and Cassie. We don't have to become real friends again, of course, but it'd be nice to get a break from the silent treatment. With everything that's happening with my parents, I don't need Cassie's sullenness to deal with too.

The minute she comes out of the bathroom, I decide to be Tamika-brave and not think about it too much.

"So, the party was today, right?" I try as she gets into bed. "Did you get to at least tell everyone why you're not there?"

She doesn't say anything, just holds up the remote and flips through the channels.

"I'm sure everyone missed you. I bet you'll have a ton of texts tomorrow." I'm trying to keep my voice even, trying to be calm, but I feel jumpy and nervous, and even with my best efforts, my words still sound that way.

Cassie turns her head, slow, to look at me. Her lids are lowered, wary, and she's still pointing the remote at the television.

"Do me a favor, Lana, okay?"

"Sure." Finally, she's talking to me. Maybe it is as simple as this.

Her voice is as cold as the kitchen floor with no socks on in winter: "Rule Number Thirteen is, Don't Act Like You Care."

The only thing—the only thing—that makes the next morning any good is that today, finally, we'll get to Maine, and tonight I will catch the Magic Moment. I'll wish my mom better, and Cassie can wish whatever she wants with her friends, and then we can head back home and this whole thing will be over. It's not how I wanted to feel at the end of this trip, but based on how it's gone, I'll take what I can get. Cassie can hate me all she wants. I just can't wait to get to the End of the Road.

After the long, long treks we've had over the last couple of days, seven hours in the car feels almost like nothing. It helps too that Grandma Tess has gotten excited again, knowing how close we are. We drive through Massachusetts and a little bit of New Hampshire, and then finally we're crossing the big, green bridge from Portsmouth into Kittery.

Grandma Tess honks the car horn three times. "Hello, Maine!" she sings, rolling down the window and waving a hand out into the sunshine. Even the air that pours into the car feels brighter, fresher, and more magical. Finally, we're here.

There are still several towns to drive through, of course, but Grandpa Howe has a story about each one. If it's not somewhere he's been, it's somewhere someone he's known has lived, or died, or done something crazy in, and I lean in close to listen to every tale.

It's almost four when we arrive at the small house Grandpa Howe rented online. It isn't the End of the Road, but it's still along the same beach where you catch the Magic Moment. The best part is, Cassie and I get our own rooms. Mine's not a lot bigger than a closet, with the ceiling sloping so low over the bed I have to be careful not to bump my head, but at least now I can close the door and be away from her. Even better? We have a real kitchen, and there's a sliding glass door that opens straight onto a wide porch, and then the beach.

Grandma Tess goes from room to room, opening all the windows, smiling bigger with each burst of ocean air that wafts in. She took her shoes off immediately and dances now on tiptoe between the rooms, twirling and humming, and kissing Grandpa Howe on the cheek every time she passes.

"I don't know, Howie." She gazes out our kitchen

window to the heavily treed front yard. "We may just have to buy this little house and move here."

Grandpa Howe teases her about how she's too spoiled by California weather to make it in Maine, and she snaps him with a dish towel.

"Speaking of spoiled," he says, dodging, "it's been almost two weeks since I cooked a good meal. I need to make sure I haven't forgotten how."

"Can we bake chocolate chip cookies?" I ask. Grandpa Howe is an expert at baking everything, but his chocolate chip cookies are so delicious, we often eat half a batch of the raw dough before we even turn on the oven.

"Mind reader," Grandpa Howe says. "And that's just the first course."

I smile and curl against his strong arm, glad at least *he* hasn't forgotten our pacts.

Cassie and Grandma Tess stay behind while we go shopping. Grandma Tess wants to write a few postcards to friends, and Cassie is sulking in her room. She's still up there with the door closed when Grandpa Howe and I get back. Not that I'm surprised. She ignores the smell of the first perfect batch of cookies, and only comes out when Grandpa Howe calls us to the table for his amazing dinner of mussels over pasta, with a crisp, fresh salad I helped make.

She disappears again as soon as we've finished clearing the table, but I decide not to let it bother me. We're all finally *here*. No more hotels, no more long hours in the car. Grandma Tess is rinsing dishes and putting them in the dishwasher, and Grandpa Howe has another sheet of cookies in the oven. The sun has gone down, and the sky is the deep, dark blue of promise. The rising moon is a little more than half-full, and even just standing on our porch, five fireflies flick on the edges of my vision. A small breeze lifts my bangs, and thrilled little goose bumps race over my whole body.

It's time.

I tell Grandpa Howe I'd like to go down to the beach, if that's okay. He's pouring wine for Grandma Tess, looking more relaxed and happy than he has all trip.

"Do you want company?" he asks, handing Grandma Tess her glass.

Part of me does want Grandpa Howe to come, so he can help me know when I really catch the Magic Moment. Still, something inside tells me I need to do this alone.

"I'll be okay. And I won't be long."

"Don't get snapped up by any mermaids." He winks.

"Howie," Grandma Tess scolds. "Everyone knows they only come out at the full moon."

Grandpa Howe laughs and says we'll have more cookies

when I get back, and as I open the sliding glass door to the beach, it feels as though I'm sliding back the curtain between my old, sad life where my mom is sick—and I'm sick inside all the time with worry for her—and the new, healthy one this wish is about to make.

Ten minutes later, though, it's still not happening. I've practiced catching and releasing three different fireflies, and I've already seen two shooting stars. The tide is glowing weirdly with clouds of stirred-up phosphorescence, and even the wind smells like magic.

The problem is, I can't skip the stone. Not even two hops. The beach is covered with dozens of perfect rocks that fit right between my pointer finger and thumb, but hard as I try, most of them sink into the water without jumping once. I knew catching the Magic Moment isn't something just anyone can do, but everything leading up to now has felt so right, and there isn't anyone else besides me who needs it more.

I try again, but the disappointing *plunk* of my rock disappearing among the ripples makes my pulse beat harder in my throat. This has to happen. It *has* to. If it doesn't, I'm sure my mom's going to die. That's been the main— the only—reason I've needed so badly to get here, and if I can't make this wish, not only will my mom not get better, but then I'll have ruined things for Cassie—and lost her friendship forever—for no reason at all.

I take a deep breath, picking up another flat rock. "You must do the thing you think you cannot do," I whisper into the beachy night air. I pretend I'm Tamika, and that I don't hear how shaky my voice sounds. I grip the skipping stone in my palm: oval, smooth, heavy as a roll of pennies, and give it a flick.

Fail, again.

Determined—both to do this and not to cry—I hunt for another perfect stone. When I find it, I stand as tall as I can, feeling the hard, pebbly beach under the thin soles of my flip-flops. I look out across the water for the spot where I think my rock will hit on its seventh skip. I visualize each of the necessary jumps, concentrating on the weight in my fingers. I bend my wrist and rotate it back and forth once, twice. On the third time I let go, pulling my arm around with as much force as I can.

I watch as my rock skips: once, twice, three times, then four.

But it doesn't come back up.

Overhead, there's the faint trail of another shooting star I've missed.

I sink to the cool, damp shore, not believing. I curl my fingers deep into the ground, grabbing up gritty handfuls and throwing them as hard as I can. Watching the pathetic little ripples they make, anger, disappointment, and three kinds of sadness roll through my stomach and my chest, up my throat, and take over my whole face. I've tried so hard—so hard—to be strong when I thought I couldn't be, to do all the right things for my parents, and Cassie, and Grandpa Howe and Grandma Tess. Now I'm here, and I still can't do it. I can't do any of this right at all.

Chapter Thirty

Cassie

I didn't tell anyone—there isn't anyone to tell—but last night, when we got to the hotel in Skenetta-whatever, I turned off my phone again. The party was over by then, and I still hadn't heard from anyone. Kendra Mack had nothing to say when I told her I didn't really have a crush on Cory Baxter, and not even Izzy Gathing had a put-down about it. No one responded either to the group text I sent—**Miss you guys so much! Have a great time!**—in hopes that at least one person would write back.

Not a single word, all day long.

So I turned it off. I didn't want it reminding me of all the fun I wasn't having, the world I was losing. Or the one I'd already lost, with Fiona, when all of this started.

I didn't turn it on again until I was in the safety of my little room at the house in Maine. When it finally *bing*ed and buzzed with messages ringing in, a surprised little laugh came out of my mouth. Maybe they really were sorry I wasn't there. Maybe my life wasn't over.

But it was only photos Kendra Mack sent to all of us of everyone posing together around the pool without me. Those, and a message from Izzy Gathing: **You should've been there. But then again, it's not like we really missed you.**

I decide to call Kendra Mack direct, to see what my fate really is.

"Hi, Cassie Parker!" she says when she answers.

"Hi, Kendra Mack."

"Did you see the pictures?"

"I did, thanks. And I'm still so sorry I couldn't come. We're in Maine now, though, and it's totally gorgeous. Like the coast of Australia or something." At least, I think it might look like that. It's too dark now to tell.

"Oh," she says, dismissing it.

"So how did things go?" I ask.

"Well, you kind of had to be there." She tells me about Perez Joynanda and Harper Warren showing up in inappropriate bathing suits, and I pretend to be shocked. "It was all I could do to get my mom not to send them home.

I only invited them because Billy Keegan asked me to, but I won't be making that mistake again."

"Yeah." I laugh, trying to do it in a throaty way that masks my shakiness. She's chatting away like everything's fine, but I'm still uncertain. "Just like I won't make the mistake again of telling you about a crush. Even a fake one. You guys got pretty carried away."

"Are you still thinking about that?" Her voice rises an octave and then falls. "Obviously you were kidding. That was days ago, anyway. Just Izzy Gathing bored with her brother's phone."

I feel the blood drain from my face. I knew that was what had been happening, but until now I didn't Know It.

"It was totally fun while it lasted, though, right?" she says. "When you sent the picture of that tacky little arcade? And your dorky selfie? Totally priceless. We were cracking up for hours."

I'm more embarrassed than I thought possible. The only solace I feel is at least the conversation's about to be over. All I have to do is laugh it off, wind things down, and—

"Wait," Kendra Mack gasps. "You're not really in like with Cory Baxter, are you? That's not why you're calling me now, right? Because then I would feel *so* bad."

I swallow hard. I can't tell whether or not she means that. I can't tell if she suspects the truth but is pretending

I'm in on the joke. Maybe she's trying to get me to confess, so she can use it against me more.

All I know is, a real friend wouldn't do any of this. I need to get off the phone with Kendra Mack this minute.

"No, of course not," I say, hoping it sounds true.

"Well," she says, "thank goodness you were kidding, because I think Gates Morrill has a crush on you. He was asking about you a lot at the party."

I make some kind of neutral noise, but I would never have a crush on a boy like Gates, real or fake. He's just an obnoxious rich kid who doesn't care about anything but himself. Fiona was right about him, for sure.

And really, I think, she was right about Kendra Mack and everyone else too. She may even have been right about me.

"I have to go," I say.

"Oh. Well, when will you be back?" Kendra Mack asks.

I realize I don't even care. "I'm not sure. We're staying here a few days, and it's a long way back to California."

"Okay. Stay in touch, I guess," she chirps.

"Yeah," I say, but my thumb's already pressed end.

It's dark outside, but I need to move around, get some fresh air, and I need to think. In the living room, Nono and Howie are sipping wine and playing Othello together. Lana isn't anywhere.

"Cassie, are you all right? You look like you've seen a ghost," Nono says.

"I think I need to take a walk."

Howie looks back toward the sliding glass door. "You just missed Lana. Probably catch her if you head out now."

I slip on my flip-flops and step outside, where the air is breezy and welcoming. The sky is not-yet-black indigo, and tons of stars are twinkling. I choose a random direction and walk toward the sound of the water.

"She was pretending," I tell myself, testing it out. "She knew all along that you really liked Cory, and she's just trying to play you more. They've been laughing at you this whole time, and they're only going to keep laughing."

I walk along the shore, thinking that over, my hands jammed into the pockets of my cardigan. The idea of it is terrible, but not being able to know either way feels worse.

"But if that were true, she would've been meaner on the phone," I argue back. "Everything's fine. She genuinely missed you at the party, and she's still your friend."

I stop, right there in the middle of the beach.

"But that's not the kind of friend you want," I say.

I stare out across the water, its rippling surface sparkling with moonlight. My whole friendship with Kendra Mack has been full of lies—lies I've told and lies I've gone along with to keep up with her group. There's so much I've been pretending, I'm not sure I even know what's real. And I don't want to do it anymore. I want to be around friends who are honest, even if I don't always like what they have to say.

Like Lana, I think. Who's only kept secrets from me because I was too self-absorbed to listen to her.

"Lana?" I ask out into the dark beach.

Lana didn't tell me the truth about her mom, but I haven't told her the truth either. I said last night she shouldn't act like she cared, but Lana cares about everything. She hasn't been pretending—I have. Pretending I'm mad when I'm not, that I don't have a crush when I really do and I have a boyfriend when I don't, pretending I like things that I think are stupid, just so I can pretend I'm as popular and perfect as Kendra Mack or Tom.

Ever since Fiona lost her diary—maybe even before that—I'm the one who's been selfish. And I want, more than anything, to stop.

I turn back toward the house, walking at first, then running.

"Lana?" I call again, searching the beach while also keeping an eye on the rocky ground in front of me.

I pass the house where we're staying and keep going. Lana's out here somewhere, I can feel it. And something tells me she needs me right now, as much as I need her.

I hear her before I see her, crying like her heart is broken.

"Cassie?" she says as I get closer, more sob than question.

And then I spot her, crumpled in a heap not far from the gently lapping water.

"What are you doing?" I crouch down.

"Nothing," she moans. "I'm trying, but I just can't." She shakes her head and wipes her face. "I'm sorry."

"What's the matter?" I ask.

She tosses a rock into the ocean, making twinkling ripples that glow with sparkly white dots. "Aren't you more worried about your other friends?" she says.

I wince, but I know I deserved that. I'm not going to pretend I don't.

"Listen, Lana. I've been terrible, and I'm sorry. I should have realized it long ago, but those people back home aren't my real friends. I've been pretending they are, because, well, that's not important right this minute. What's important is that you're upset, and I'm here, and Rule Number Fourteen is going to be No More Pretending, Period. I know about your mom. I know there are things you've needed to share, and I haven't let you. But I want to listen. You're always so smart, and strong when you say things right out. I like you so much that way. So I want you to trust me, and do it now. I promise I will, too."

I'm not sure what she thinks about all that at first, but in the moonlight, and the spooky lit-up ocean, I see one half of her mouth lift in a smile.

That makes me smile, too.

She rubs her nose with the back of her hand and straightens up. "Rule Number Fifteen has to be You'll Tell Me Later What Really Happened at Kendra Mack's Pool Party, though."

"I promise, I'll tell you, but this feels more important. You've been acting like nothing's wrong, and if anyone knows how terrible that feels, it's me."

She looks at me with a question in her eyes before staring across the water. Maybe she's remembering all the ways I haven't exactly earned her trust. I'm afraid she's going to brush me off, but instead she lets out a quivery breath, and starts.

It takes a long time, and there's a lot of crying in between. She tells me about her mom's headaches and naps—having to tiptoe around the house, pretending her mom's just a little tired, or a little stressed. She tells me about having to do more around the house and not getting as much attention, and how mad she's been about her parents not trusting her with the truth. How wrong it feels to be mad at someone who's sick. She talks about what she's afraid of—brain damage from the surgery, or worse, cancer and her mom dying. She says her parents are so close that sometimes they forget to include her. Or that they treat her like a grown-up, which she likes most of the time, except for when she just wants to be coddled instead of having to act so mature. She tells me she worries a lot, but that she feels like she can't share that with her parents or even our grandparents, because she doesn't want to be one more person for them to worry about.

"But it's their job to worry about you," I say.

"I know." She sighs. "But the way our family is—it's kind of my job to take care of them, too."

"If you're busy with that, though, and they're busy with taking care of each other, who's taking care of you?"

She smiles sadly and shrugs.

"There's Nono," I say. "And Grandpa Howe." It's what Lana calls him, but even in my voice now, it sounds right.

"They take care of me, of course, but ever since the wedding I haven't wanted to be a third wheel. I know they love me, but they love each other, too, and I feel like I should—"

I grab her by the shoulders. "You should lean on me, then."

"But you live hours away." She starts to cry again.

I stand up and face the ocean. "We'll figure that out.

Rule Number Sixteen is From Now On, It's You and Me No Matter What, and I'm going to prove it. So, what's the problem here?"

She reaches for a rock and stands too. "I can't get the stone to skip seven times. I've gotten the firefly, and there've been a dozen shooting stars, but this part"—she gestures feebly with the round, flat stone—"I just can't do it."

The Magic Moment. Of course. I take the stone from her hand. I've never skipped rocks before—I haven't even seen anyone do it in real life, since Tom prefers books and skateboards—but it happens all the time in TV and the movies. It can't be that hard. Only, maybe it is, if Lana's been out here trying all this time and can't. Chances are, I won't be able to do it either.

I'm just going to try my best, for my friend. My true friend.

"Okay." I take in a breath and grip the cool, smooth stone in my hand. I cock back my wrist and give it a toss. It sinks immediately.

I pick up another one and try it again. Lana, rigid and hopeful, counts the splashes under her breath.

One.

Two-Three.

Four.

Five-Six-Seven.

"You did it!" She claps.

I can't believe it either.

"Now the firefly," I say fast.

She stumbles after one of at least a dozen glowing around us. I'm not sure, but they didn't seem to be there before.

"Got it." She clasps her hands together, holds it for a heartbeat, and lets it go.

"Now look up." She moves back over to me. We stand together, the surprisingly cold water lapping our toes and our faces tipped toward the sky.

It's not pretending, I tell myself, taking Lana's hand. I'm not pretending I want this, because even though I don't really believe in the Magic Moment, Lana does, and wanting it to be true for her sake is absolutely real.

When she squeezes my hand back, two bright streaks gleam across the sky, one after the other. We gasp and look at each other in surprise.

"Quick, make a wish." Lana shuts her eyes.

I know Lana's wishing for her mom to be okay. I'd wish it too, if I doubted any of Lana's urgency. But there's another thing I want to wish for, one that she needs just as much as her mom getting better—and that I need too.

I wish to be, and have, real friends like Lana—and not the pretending kind—for the rest of my life, forever.

I open my eyes, and the shooting stars have vanished. Even the moonlight on the ocean seems less bright, and the rippling phosphorescence has disappeared. It's probably just my imagination, but it seems suddenly there are fewer fireflies, too.

"Thanks for coming to find me," Lana says as we turn to head back up the beach.

"Well, I couldn't leave you out here to get snapped up by mermaids, could I?"

She gives me a little shove toward the water. "You don't think I really believe *that* part, do you?"

"Well . . ." I bend to scoop up a handful of ocean, my fingers leaving white glitter streaks behind. I toss it at her, and she squeals even though I miss. "You sure do have Grandpa Howe fooled!"

Chapter Thirty-One

Lana

We decide to stay in our little cottage three more days—days full of playing board games and walking on the beach, cooking, napping, dancing around the house, writing postcards back home, reading books together, eating cookies, and exploring little towns on the coastline. Grandpa Howe walks us to the End of the Road, and when Grandma Tess goes up and knocks on the door, the couple living there for the summer is happy to give us a tour. There's been a lot of renovation done since he sold it, Grandpa Howe tells us, but it's still amazing to see the rooms and the wide porch I've heard so many stories about. Grandma Tess gets so fired up, she decides to forget about wishing for a place to all be together in

California and wants to find one right here. So we follow other neighborhood roads, looking for FOR SALE signs and dreaming about the perfect vacation place. Best of all, we spend a lot of time around the table, or on the porch, or on a blanket, telling stories.

Cassie and I, of course, tell Grandpa Howe and Grandma Tess everything about the Magic Moment, which includes me opening up about my hard feelings around Mom's sickness. This turns into a surprising conversation about fears, which includes Grandma Tess telling the story of how scared she was when Cassie's mom was born, even surrounded by all her commune friends, and Grandpa Howe talking more about when Nana Lilia died.

"It felt wrong," he says, "to be sad about our wonderful life together: my success at work and our beautiful family. After she was gone, though, all I could think about were those trips we'd postponed until retirement. All those adventures we never had."

Grandma Tess suggests that sometimes adventure might be overrated.

"I'm still looking forward to many, many more, of course," she says, "but it wasn't until I met you that I really felt I had a home, Howie. I didn't even realize I'd been missing one." She holds out her hands like she's giving us all a surprise. "Even the things you most want to turn out a certain way often don't. But that doesn't mean that the ways they do turn out aren't good."

Grandpa Howe squeezes Grandma Tess around the shoulders and presses a kiss between her cheek and ear. "Even terrible losses can lead you to some nice gifts, I'll give you that."

"Best you can do," she says, kissing him back, "is love yourself and the people around you as much as you can, in all the ways you can find."

Under the table, Cassie gives my leg a little kick, and we smile at each other.

On the day of Mom's surgery, Grandpa Howe wakes me up with chocolate chip pancakes cut in the shapes of stars and sprinkled with confectioner's sugar, which I know is a reminder about my wish, and how he hopes it will come true, too. Before I even eat, though, I call Mom and Dad. In part it's to say one more time how much I love them before they head to the hospital, but I also want to tell them something else. Thanks to Cassie, I've learned that it is better to say things straight out, and it's time for me to do that with my parents.

When I get them both on the call, I explain that I know they haven't wanted me to be scared, but not talking about things has made them scarier. That, and it's made me feel left out.

"It's like you two have had this big secret together that you've wanted to keep from me," I admit.

"Oh, Lana," Dad says. "That's not been it at all. You haven't had many questions, so we thought you didn't want to know. But we should have checked in more, and I'm sorry. You're just so mature all the time; sometimes we forget."

Mom cries a little, and Dad won't stop apologizing, but telling them everything feels a lot better. Dad assures me that Mom's procedure is a common one considering how serious it is, and isn't so dangerous that she might die during the operation. He agrees to keep me posted all day on her progress.

"I'm scared too, of course," he admits. "We still don't know what the tumor is exactly, and whether it's cancer or not, the recovery could take a long time. But your mom is strong, and I know we'll all be together through it, which is what matters."

Mom admits it's been harder than she expected for me to be away while all of this has been going on. "You were being so brave about it, though, Lana. And I never want to stand in the way of your experiences, whether I'm sick or not. This trip is one of those, but perhaps my illness was one, too. I didn't think about it that way before."

Dad thanks me for telling them my real feelings and

helping them understand. I realize I feel lighter in my heart and my body. Maybe trying to avoid your fears instead of facing them might sometimes be worse.

"That sounded like a good conversation," Grandpa Howe says when I'm done.

I give a grateful smile to him and Cassie, who's come into the kitchen at the sound of our voices and the smell of pancakes.

"It might even top this breakfast," I tell him.

Grandpa Howe ruffles the top of my head. "You know what? I'll take that."

"Well, in that case"—Cassie reaches for my fork—"I'll be taking these." She scoops up a bite of buttery, chocolaty, syrupy goodness and stuffs it into her grinning mouth.

Later that afternoon, when Mom's safely out of surgery and resting well, and we find out for sure that the tumor was *not* cancerous, Grandpa Howe takes us all out for victory ice cream, and we head down to the beach. The water's a little cold for me and Cassie to stand for very long, so we stretch out on our towels in the sun.

Right away, Cassie says, "I did something terrible, but I'm not sure how to fix it. I've been waiting to tell you until we knew your mom was okay."

I squint at her. "Well, I think the last couple of days

272

have proved one of the best ways to make something better is to talk about it, right?"

She smiles out the side of her mouth. "Why do you think I'm bringing it up?"

We lean back on our elbows, watching the water, as she tells me about her friend Fiona, and what happened with Kendra Mack and Fiona's diary. How Cassie and Fiona haven't spoken since the whole mess, and Cassie knows the not-speaking is a big part her fault. She feels terrible about it but doesn't know how to win Fiona back. At first Cassie was too embarrassed and mad at Fiona to even want to try, but now that she sees the whole situation differently, she's worried it's too late.

To me, though, it doesn't seem that complicated.

I shrug. "Tell her what you just told me."

Cassie chews her lip. "But in Fiona's eyes, Kendra Mack is—the worst. That I became friends with her? And treated Fiona the same way they used to treat us? She probably felt terrible when she found out who had her diary. And there I was, for weeks after, laughing and talking with the same girl."

"Well, you miss Fiona, right? It took you a while to realize it, but you do. And I bet she misses you too. Probably by now she's also had time to realize it, like you have. Sometimes you need that—space to be angry and then not anymore. Like when we were mad at each other on the way here. We were together all the time, but we still weren't ready to talk. Being shoved together might've even made it worse."

She looks at me. "That's true."

"So, why would it be different for you and Fiona?"

"Because—"

I put my hand gently over her mouth. "Just call her, Cassie. It's like this Chinese proverb Tamika likes: 'A journey of a thousand miles begins with a single step.'"

"Oh, Tamika," she says, the words muffled by my hand. "One day I gotta meet that girl."

The idea of Cassie meeting Tamika, and me meeting Fiona, gets more exciting when Cassie finally calls Fiona and apologizes. I don't hear the conversation, because Cassie wanted to have it on her own, but when she's done, she thanks me and says they have plans to go roller-skating together when Cassie gets back.

"It's an activity we can have fun doing even if the talking part isn't so great," Cassie explains. "Because I know it'll take a while to get back to where we were."

It's clear by the sound of her voice that she's hopeful they'll still get there. When I tell her I wish I could be there for moral support, she shrugs and suggests I come down some other weekend, after she and Fiona are better. Unlike the dodgy way she's acted before, I know this time Cassie means it, and it's an exciting thing to look forward to.

The next day we have to do everything—swimming, walking on the beach, watching the sunset from our porch—all for the last time. We map out our return trip, deciding that even though Chicago might be fun to revisit one day, we want to get as much out of our adventure as possible and will start a completely different route in the morning.

Before we know it, Grandma Tess is starting a new playlist and steering us toward New Hampshire. It's good Cassie and I will have so much time in the car together, because we need to work on another plot. This time it's not about stealing Cassie's phone back or turning the car around, but what Cassie should do about Kendra Mack.

"That girl deserves some of her own medicine," I say. "Not to mention you need to break from her for good."

Cassie tries to convince me that Kendra Mack thought Cassie was in on the joke, but when we review all Cassie's messages, it's impossible to believe Kendra Mack's total innocence.

It takes us until Columbus, Ohio, to fully devise the whole plan.

"You're sure about this?" Cassie asks me, taking my

phone from my hand. After some back-and-forth about other ideas, I decided we should stop trying to come up with a new plan and instead just steal Kendra's.

"Absolutely." I nod.

We're in the courtyard at the Easton Town Center, where Grandma Tess suggested, that after two weeks with the same clothes, we could all use a new outfit injection. Cassie and I found semi-matching sundresses immediately, but Grandma Tess and Grandpa Howe are taking their time browsing.

Cassie had told me she suspected part of why Kendra Mack was even friends with her in the first place was because Kendra had a crush on Tom. If Kendra Mack and Izzy Gathing could pretend to be a boy, Cassie and I certainly could, too, though it wouldn't take much to write texts better than theirs.

"Okay, but if Tom finds out, he's going to kill me. He thinks Kendra Mack is obnoxious," she says.

"Well, I agree she's obnoxious—"

Cassie play-slaps me on the arm.

"But we're not going to *say* they're from him," I remind her. "We're just going to let her think it's true, and watch her go crazy. This way, it's still her own fault. She'll never *really* know what happened, but she'll be too embarrassed to ask you about it. It's not as awful as what she did to you either, because no one will ever know about it except her and us."

A smile flickers in Cassie's eyes, but then she frowns again. "How are we going to make sure she doesn't do something irrational, like call your number a thousand times or crash my family's Labor Day party?"

Her anxiousness reminds me of myself at the beginning of this trip, wondering how quickly we were going to become best friends, and how to make certain we would have the most magical vacation ever. How I planned I was going to keep all my fear inside myself, and be so strong it would somehow make my mom better. I think about how those things have still sort of happened, but like Grandma Tess said, not always in the ways I thought they should.

"I don't know if we can make sure of anything," I tell Cassie, "especially where Kendra Mack is concerned—"

She snorts in agreement.

"But I know we'll work through all of it together."

"Absolutely," she says, wrapping her arm around my shoulder and giving me a squeeze.

Turns out, it doesn't take long for us to get bored with texting Kendra Mack, or even thinking about her. She flirted like crazy, of course, the minute she suspected it could be Tom (I'll give you a hint: You might know a girl who might be my sister, we wrote), and it was a little funny to string her along, but both of us soon felt kind of bad about what we were doing, and by the time we arrive in St. Louis, we decide to end it with a **Sorry. Wrong number.** There's a lounge with a bowling alley in the basement of our hotel, and we've got way more fun things to do down there with our grandparents. I block Kendra's number from my phone, so she can't text me anymore, and that's that.

"She's going to hate that," Cassie says as we change for our evening with Grandma Tess and Grandpa Howe. "Being ignored."

"I'm more than happy to ignore that girl for the rest of my life," I say.

Cassie smiles. "Me too."

We spend the rest of the night eating Klondike bars, fried cheese with marinara sauce, spicy-sweet spring rolls, and tiny barbecue sandwiches with coleslaw on them in between rounds of bowling. Cassie and Grandpa Howe make an even better team in the lanes than they did on the dance floor, but at least Grandma Tess and I don't get totally walloped. At nine o'clock, the regular lights go down and the disco lights come up, turning the back of the bowling alley into a neon-glowing dance floor.

"Ladies," Grandpa Howe says, extending his hand to

the open area where people are already starting to shake around.

"Don't mind if I do." Grandma Tess takes his arm. "Girls, maybe you should run up to the DJ booth and see if she'll play us 'The Hustle.' I bet we could get the whole room going." She winks and fluffs her hair as Grandpa Howe twirls her out into the crowd.

Cassie and I head over to make our request, but we ask for a couple of our own favorites, too. We've been sharing our music in the car since we left Maine, and it's been fun learning new things from her and seeing her enjoy my collection, as well. Pretty much everything we do now is better when we do it together, I think, as we start bouncing around to the music, making crazy faces. And I know even when we get back home, we'll find ways to keep having fun. Together, we'll figure out Cassie's careful truce with Fiona, my mom's long recovery, and anything else that comes our way. We'll send texts and write postcards, and whenever we can, beg for visits.

Under the swirling lights, bopping with my cousin and my grandparents, a sparkling buzzy happiness fills my chest. I know that our trip is slowly coming to an end, but the long adventure between Cassie and me is just getting started.

Acknowledgments

Thank you to my editor and longtime collaborator, Anica Mrose Rissi, for her dedication to both this project and me, and for the miles across which our friendship has stretched. Enormous gratitude also goes to my agent, Meredith Kaffel at DeFiore and Company, for being such a fantastic partner on this path; Katherine Tegen for believing in my abilities as an author; Alex Arnold for so sweetly and expertly taking care of all the details, and the rest of the folks at Katherine Tegen Books for sharing their talents in order to bring *Drive Me Crazy* to life. Thank you to Scott for traveling with me down all roads, to Amy for staying on this journey with me since we were seven, and Meg for being the best cousin on the planet. To booksellers, librarians, and teachers everywhere, thank you for all you do to match the right book to the right person. And, finally, if you are reading this book yourself—thank you the most.

Remember when Fiona's diary was stolen and read out loud on the bus?

Read on for a sneak peek at her side of the story in
This Is All Your Fault, Cassie Parker!

Chapter One

Cassie is positive we've been spotted, and slows down as though suddenly fascinated by the Hallway Etiquette poster over the water fountain. But this is the longest stretch we've ever walked undetected behind her crush, Cory Baxter (and the most conversation we've overheard between him and his friends), so I'm not letting her break this streak just because she's a little nervous. I tug a strand of her long, glossy black hair and make a "keep going" face without worrying whether or not she'll follow. I know she'll follow. Because Cassie loves the thrill of this game, too, and because she's more than a little obsessed with Cory.

She's back by my side in not even two steps, raising her eyebrows in silent "I can't believe this" excitement. We've been tracking Cory Baxter—code name: Lagoon—since we got back from spring break, when Cassie suddenly went googly-eyed in the cafeteria over him. Just like one of those old cartoons where someone gets hit in the chest by a Cupid arrow, or sniffs a love potion. It even caught *her* off guard.

But I'd had a similar feeling right before spring break myself, when Tyrick Nevin—code name: Pencil—and I were assigned to the same group for our vocabulary project. Tyrick had been in my English class all year, and was always thoughtful and quiet, but I had never considered him more than a nice classmate. Not until I was sitting across from him and realized that his eyes are a hypnotically golden color: light brown with a dark brown ring around the edge. I had never seen eyes such a color, and I found it hard to look at them and talk at the same time.

So I came up with a plan. Or rather, Cassie and I did, which is the way we always do things, ever since the summer before fifth grade when we ended up in the same week of Girls Up camp and discovered the power of our collaborations. (For one: we are great at creating obstacle courses. Two: by harnessing my problem-solving skills and Cassie's competitive streak, we can get through everyone else's the fastest too.) There have been several more revelations like this since then, all demonstrating that we are meant to be best friends. She has good ideas—I have good ideas—but somehow when we share them we both get even better ones.

Like this Cory/Tyrick thing. My original thought was that we should learn as much about both of them as we could by observation—likes, dislikes, general interests—so that when we eventually talked to either one of them, we would have something clever and pertinent to say. This was admittedly easier for me, since Tyrick is in my class. All period I would take careful mental notes about the things he said, the way he tapped his pen on the desk when he was trying to come up with a word—whatever details I could grab on to—and then record them all in my diary. But Cassie didn't have as much luck, since Cory is an eighth grader. He has online accounts in the usual places, which was exciting to discover at first, but then we realized Cassie would have to follow him to see any of his posts, which would obliterate the secret element. Nobody really puts much in the school's web roster, so that wasn't any help, either.

Which is when she decided we needed to start spying on them both.

"This is it, this is it," Cassie whispers beside me, making sure to keep her lips from moving. We're rounding the corner from the long stretch of the research wing (where

Cory and his friends hang out before school) to the high-trafficked main corridor. This is when we change directions and weave our way through the crowd to the seventh grade hall, where, if there's time, we can catch a glimpse of Tyrick by his locker before the homeroom bell rings.

Now, rather than moving into the backpack-and-braces crowd toward our own hallway, Cassie links her arm through mine, hooking me tight. Her nervousness from a few minutes ago seems to have disappeared, and the determined expression on her face is the only cue I need. We plunge across the hallway traffic and keep following Cory and his friends into the eighth grade wing. As soon as we cross the threshold into the newer, smoother hall, we swap glances, reflecting to each other the same thrill: we've never gone this far before.

For the briefest moment, I'm disappointed I won't get an early peek at Pencil today—I like to know what he's wearing, in case it's one of the outfits he looks the best in, so I can prepare my face before I get to English class—but when Cassie gets that mischievous glint in her eye (the one that reminds me so much of her feisty grandmother, Tess), something fun is always going to follow.

Ahead of us, Cory waves bye to his friends—Jeannette (not his girlfriend, we were happy to discover), and Hopper (we don't know much about him other than he is Cory's favorite partner for some magic game that involves a lot of trading cards)—as they both enter the first classroom on our left. Now Cory is completely alone, and as far as we can tell, has no idea we're following him. Our arms are still linked, and Cassie squeezes mine between her jabby elbow and her rib cage. I can feel the vibrations of adrenaline rising in us both. There are still plenty of older kids out in the hall, so if Cory turned around he wouldn't exactly spot us, but the homeroom bell will be ringing in only a couple more minutes. We also have no idea where he's going, or how far.

But Cassie isn't slowing down, so I'm dying to see what she's going to do. From the way she's nibbling the edge of her lower lip, I can tell she is too.

Two doors farther, Cory ducks into his homeroom class: *Ms. Cruik, History*, the sign outside the door says. To my surprise and shock, Cassie follows him in, slipping her arm out from mine and sweeping her hair in one smooth, confident gesture over her shoulder. Cassie marches straight to Ms. Cruik's desk at the front of the room, and I have no choice but to follow, mainly because I have to hear what she's going to say.

It takes Ms. Cruik a moment to look up from her desk computer, but when she does, Cassie lights up her best, most teacher-charming smile.

"Hi, Ms. Cruik."

"It's 'cruck,' actually," the teacher says. "Like 'cluck' with an *r* instead of an *l*."

"Oh. Well, I'm sorry, Ms. Cruik"—she mimics the teacher's pronouncement perfectly, including the note of suspicion—"but learning more about upper-grade teachers is actually why we're here. My name's Cassie Parker, and my friend Fiona and I are having a hard time deciding which, um"—she glances at the whiteboard, obviously trying to remember what classroom we're in—"history class would be best for us next year. We know we don't have much control, but we'd like to know what to hope for."

Ms. Cruik is still doubtful, but she does straighten up a little.

"We're just wondering what you intend for students to gain by taking this class," Cassie continues.

Now Ms. Cruik's face transforms from distrustful to impressed.

"Well, Cassie, I'm happy to help. I hope that when they leave my class my students have a better understanding of the complex tapestry of American history, and become more intellectually enriched citizens because of it."

Cassie smiles. "Thank you, Ms. Cruik. Fiona, you've got that?"

"Um. Of course." I slide a notepad out of my book bag and dig for a pen. Over our heads, the homeroom bell chimes its ugly digital tone.

"Oh gosh," Cassie says, looking at the clock in mock horror. "I didn't realize we were going to be late. Ms. Cruik, I hate to impose, but do you mind giving us a pass? We have to get back to the seventh grade wing."

It's clear Ms. Cruik doesn't quite think our little poll is worthy of a hall pass. She glances at her still-chattering homeroom, though, and makes the decision that it's better to get us out of here and begin announcements rather than lecture us on time management.

The second her door shuts behind us, Cassie and I speed-walk down the now-empty eighth grade hallway, hands clamped over our mouths to keep our giggles from bursting out. The moment we're in the main hall, safely far away from Ms. Cruik's room or Cory's ears, we both jump up and down, squealing and talking over each other.

"I can't believe you did that!"

"I can't believe I just did that!"

"She had no idea you were faking."

"Do you think he was watching? I was too nervous to look around. But we were there! *In his homeroom class!*"

"You were so calm! I had no idea what you were going to say."

"I know! Me neither!"

We straighten and quiet down when one of the secretaries comes out of the staff bathroom farther down the hall. Both of us make sure to clutch our hall passes in clear sight as we start walking again.

"It's not a bad idea, though," I consider.

"What?"

"Polling more eighth grade teachers. I thought her answer was pretty good."

"Ugh." Cassie flicks her fingers in the air, dismissing it. "Her class sounds so boring. Besides, we already know whatever teachers Kendra Mack and Izzy Gathing sign up for next year are the ones we really want. And anyway, now we don't need to poll anybody else because we know Lagoon's homeroom!"

We're almost to our own homerooms ourselves, so I decide not to tell Cassie that I'm probably interested in the exact opposite classes that Kendra or her friends will be taking. For now, I don't want to ruin this fun.

"It still might be useful for future spy tactics," I say instead.

"True," she agrees. "Talk about it at lunch?"

I nod. She waves her pass at me with a sneaky wink, and I can't help grinning back.

Dear Diary:

What an up-and-down roller coaster of a day. I'm eager to slip into bed and get on my way to a new morning, but so much happened that I need to get it all straight in my head. Things started out fun this morning, with stalking Lagoon and <u>getting into his homeroom</u> (!!!). Cassie was brilliant as usual. It almost makes me sad that school's over soon and there'll be no more Pencil or Lagoon for a while, but at least we'll have the super-amazing Disneyland trip with Dad and Leelu to look forward to. (Which reminds me, Cassie and I need to look at the website and see what new rides there are since the last time both our families went.)

But anyway, then in third period—you won't believe it—<u>Pencil turned right around in his seat to talk to me before English class!</u> In that dreamy, Michael Bublé voice of his (extra low because he was trying not to be too loud, but still had to be heard over everyone getting out their books), he said, "Hey, Fiona. Are you okay?" My first instinct was to check my shirt to see if there were leftover breakfast bits on me, or if my arms had exploded in dripping pustules, but then he said, "I just didn't see you this morning like usual, so I wondered if you had an appointment." He wondered! If I had an appointment! <u>Because he didn't see me before school.</u> Which means he has been noticing me in the morning as much as I am noticing him!!! Diary, it was ten thousand vocabulary words at once: exalting, electrifying, astonishing, breathtaking, wondrous, and addictive. I could hardly concentrate on our out-loud reading in class, but when it got to my turn I read each word aiming my voice at the back of Pencil's head, hoping it might make him turn around again and look at me with those eyes.

So, of course I was dying to see Cassie at lunch, and when I told her my news, her mouth dropped open in a satisfyingly shocked smile. We bounced in our chairs about a zillion times—I'm surprised we didn't knock something over with how hard the table was vibrating.

But then her voice dropped and her expression changed. She said she needed good news, because her morning had been so depressing. I went straight into listening mode, thinking maybe it was about a grade, but instead she narrated this long thing about Neftali (in case you need a reminder: the prettiest one in Kendra's clan), some eighth grade boy named Carter, and him standing her up. Cassie seemed so serious about it, but by the time she finished, really it just sounded like Neftali misinterpreted some texts. When I asked her why she cared so much about a girl who didn't even know we existed, Cassie got that haughty, dismissive look on her face and muttered something about *how we could be as popular next year and she's just trying to do research. And get this, Diary—the way she found out the whole Neftali thing? She <u>followed</u> the two of them down the hall just like we do with Pencil and Lagoon! She said since it worked so well this morning, she wanted to try it again.*

Which—I have a lot to say about, including how disappointed I was that she used something of <u>ours</u> to get information about <u>them</u>. I knew, though, if I said anything else, she'd give me the snotty silent treatment through science class, and I didn't want to ruin the good parts of the morning, but I just don't understand Cassie's fixation on those girls. Like the thing she said this morning about taking whatever classes they were signing up for. The last thing I want is to be anywhere near those spoiled show-offs. Yes, Cassie's always been interested in clothes and having a good reputation, but that's what I like about her—her emphasis on <u>good</u> reputation, not <u>popular</u> reputation. And she's never been so focused on her looks that she can barely think about anything else. At the end of lunch I swear she checked her lip gloss five times before we got up from the table. I tell you, I would rather listen to my uncles talking about yard work, watch Frozen with Leelu for the 7,321st time, do an entire worksheet of multiplying by fractions, or have to sit through an embarrassing *biology video more than talk about Neftali or Kendra. And definitely more than watching Cassie adjust her makeup.*

We turned it around like we always do (on the way to science I asked her how our morning discoveries will change our spying, and she had lots to say about that), but it left a sour feeling in my heart.

Which (sorry for the long entry) made it even harder than usual to fake excitement when Jennifer came over again tonight. As if she hadn't already dominated this weekend, which, as you know, was supposed to be just us and Dad. She'd bought me and Leelu our own copy of Inside Out *(the DVD has extra stuff on it you can't get from a download), and I admit it was super nice of her to remember how much Leelu and I loved it in the theater, but when it got to the part where the first island starts collapsing, instead of grabbing for my hand, Leelu crawled right up into Jennifer's lap. Jennifer slid her hand along the sofa cushions to try and hold mine as well, but I pretended I was too wrapped up in the movie to notice, mainly because some kind of island was crumbling inside of me at the same time. How could I hold hands with her? During a movie that's Leelu's and mine? Especially when we only met her four months ago? And suddenly my sister is all cuddly with her instead of me? I wanted to text Mom about it, but around the subject of Jennifer she stiffly says*

Dad has every right to be happy. She's not the one who's getting this total stranger forced on her all the time, though. She doesn't have to pretend to be excited about a person she barely knows or likes, just because her dad (and now her sister) is all gaga.

It feels a lot better to tell you that, at least. Dad and Mom are so civil all the time, it's like I'm not allowed to have bad feelings. Luckily, I have Cassie, who's pretty much the only one who understands me. For now, thanks for being there, Diary. Hope it's a better report tomorrow.

Yours,

Fiona

Chapter Two

Cassie does help make things better in the morning. Before I've even washed my face, my phone is lit up with a bunch of emojis and Cassie's new plans for our stalking route. Now that we know Tyrick really is looking for me, she decides we need to start our morning patrol in our own hall, going first to her locker (because she has a mirror we can angle so that we spot Tyrick before he sees us) and then to mine (for which we have to walk past his), even if we don't need anything out of them.

Then to the library to stare at Lagoon, she messages.

Okay meet you at the bus drop-off, I tell her, hurrying down to get breakfast. Weeks when we stay at Mom's, she takes both Leelu and me to school, but at Dad's we have to ride the bus. It isn't the worst thing on the planet, but I don't think anyone in the history of middle school has ever enjoyed it.

Did things go okay last night? Cassie messages when I get to my bus stop.

Leelu likes Jennifer a lot more than I do, I admit.

Well she does bring you guys a lot of presents. Brainwashing, you know.

I smile a little at that. Cassie was the greatest friend ever last year when Mom and Dad told us they couldn't live together anymore. She helped me pack when Mom moved into the condo and we sold our house (Dad and Mom explained it would be better for Leelu and me to live somewhere that wasn't full of old memories), and helped me decorate my room in Dad's new place. If it hadn't been for her, Leelu, and the elaborate Nicholas Sparks–inspired story I wrote in my diary about my parents getting back together (even though they said it would never happen), I don't think I'd have survived. That Cassie isn't immediately trying to make me adore Jennifer like everyone else is exactly the kind of comforting that makes her the best friend in the whole world.

When she hops off her bus with a big smile, we hurry to catch a glimpse of Tyrick, and my bad feelings about last night fall to the background even further. Tyrick is in one of my favorite shirts, and gives me a one-handed "Hi" as we walk by. I'm not sure who's bouncing more on the way to the library, where we'll spy on Lagoon: me or Cassie.

"You're so gonna get asked out before the end of the year," she hisses when we find a table and settle in.

I feel myself flush.

"I wonder if we could double with—oh. Six o'clock." She ducks her head and leans close to the desk, having spotted someone interesting behind me—someone other than Cory, who we already know is in the computer lab, thanks to earlier scopes, and the wall of windows between it and the library. Whoever Cassie's spotted now could have on a great outfit, or be picking their nose—it's hard to tell from her expression.

Before I can get a glance, though, my chorus friend Evie comes in with her best friend, Aja. They see us and wave, coming over to our table.

"Are you guys studying?" Evie rushes in a loud whisper. "We didn't know you hung out here. Can we study with you too? We have that math test coming up and—ooh, Fiona, I love your hair that way."

Automatically, I reach up to feel my head, making sure everything is still lying down flat. For most of the year, my hair's been a kinked-out curly crown that sproings up all around my face and ears, unlike Evie's, which she gets done into glossy spirals. I've been growing mine out, just to experiment, and now it's finally long enough to wear in a bun-looking pony if I sleek it all down tight with tons of product, lots of brushing, and what feels like a hundred bobby pins jammed into the sides. I'm constantly expecting it to turn a bit flyaway, though, and sometimes wonder if I shouldn't just cut it back.

"Huh?" Cassie snorts, her whole face tightening with criticism. "Just because Fee's got fluffiness doesn't mean she can't be sleek, too. I mean, is that such a surprise?"

It stuns me, and Evie too.

"Of course I love it natural," Evie stammers, "but this is so . . . sophisticated." She darts her eyes at me in apology.

But before I can say or do anything, Aja leans on the table with one hand, putting her body between Cassie and Evie. A wave of her spicy perfume wafts over us.

"Do you think you'll keep growing it?" she asks, as if my hair is suddenly the most interesting topic of conversation.

Aja is a tall, Egyptian-queen-looking girl, and while we know each other because of Evie and chorus, we don't normally hang out. She's perfectly nice, but somehow her closeness now is intimidating, especially since Cassie was just so horribly rude. I say something clumsy about somewhere between my chin and my shoulders, though with summer just about upon us, it might get hot.

Cassie hasn't even noticed. Her focus is back to the glass windows. Behind them in the lab, Cory must be getting ready to make his move to homeroom, because Cassie starts getting her things together so we can follow him. We can't go in there because without a coding project (only for eighth graders) we'll look too obvious, but from here we can see perfectly. Right now, I'm just glad to have a way out of this situation.

"I'll see you in chorus, okay?" I apologize to Evie and Aja with my face.

"Have a good first period," Evie chirps behind us, like everything is fine.

As we stride out of the library, Cassie super-widens her eyes so that she looks like a silly manga character, mouthing, *Have a good first period*.

Again, it's shocking.

"Hey, did something happen with Tom yesterday?" I say, careful.

She looks surprised. "No, why? Did he post something about me?"

"No. I mean, if he did, I wouldn't know. You just seem on edge today."

Mean is the word I want to use, but I need to be cautious. Cassie and her brother, Tom, have been fighting more than usual lately—or, more specifically, she's been fighting with her parents about her brother, who's older and in their eyes perfect—and sometimes it leaves her pouty and sensitive. If I'm not careful her temper will flare up from nowhere at me, and *we'll* end up in a fight.

She rolls her eyes. "Ugh. I know you like her and everything, but sometimes that Evie can be, you know."

"Can be what?" I like Evie. She's nice.

Cassie makes another sickeningly sweet face—with the emphasis on sick. "A little too much is all. She should have learned to tone down the sunshine by now. We're not in sixth grade anymore. She doesn't have to be everyone's friend."

"Well, she's my friend," I say.

She tosses me a humble shrug. "I'm glad she likes you so much, I guess," she says. "And your hair does look sophisticated that way."

It's still not much of a peace offering, but I understand it's the closest thing to an apology as I'll get right now.

"We'll see if it holds up by lunch." I smooth my hair a bit more, deciding to let the issue go. "And whether Pencil has anything to say about it."

With that, she squeaks in excitement, and we follow Cory once again into the eighth grade wing. We don't go all the way to his homeroom this time, because we can't be late again, but Cassie's thrilled anyway. I'm just glad she's happy, though when we separate for homeroom she hollers "Ciao, bella!" at me the way Kendra and all her other friends do. In a way that sounds practiced.

I can't believe it's already a mixed-up morning, or that I need my diary so soon, even for just a quick entry.

Ebullient girl
Vivacious and sweet
Interested in everyone
Even if some think it's too much.

Amazon queen
Just waiting to pounce
And silence you with her kohl-eyed stare.

Catty without cause
Always
Silently judging
So confident in her opinions
Immune to
Everyone else's.

It feels like a mean thing to write about my best friend, but also good to get down, because I don't want to dwell on negative feelings about Cassie. I decide to turn things around when I see her again at lunch.

"We need to make a list," I tell her when we get to our table.

She grins, sly. "Ways to sabotage your dad's romance?"

"Ha. Maybe tomorrow. This, you may be surprised to hear, is more important." I show her the fresh, blank page in my notebook, across the top of which I've written *PLANS FOR DISNEYLAND*.

Cassie fake swoons against her chair. "Finally my dream of freeing Aladdin from my evil twin, Jasmine, is within reach!"

"You might want to explain that little third grade infatuation to Lagoon first." I nod over at their table. We have a perfect view from here, but they can't quite see us.

"Oh, I don't know. Maybe we need a vintage Disney marathon this weekend, so I can get her moves down. I may have forgotten the best ones."

"Hopefully Jennifer won't butt in this time," I grumble.

But Cassie's not going to let me go down that path today. She pulls me up to get in line for our drinks, humming "A Whole New World" close to my ear, and doesn't even acknowledge Kendra's gang when we pass their table, or seem to care about Cory, either. When we're through the line, she does a little Wizard of Oz–style skip to our seats, and takes out her best pen to write down all our ideas: the rides we'll have to do multiple times, the ones Leelu's finally big enough to go on with us, the food we want to try, plus the shows at night we can't miss.

"And Haunted Mansion at least five times," she insists.

I cross my eyes and make my face like a cartoon ghost's. "Of course!"

As the list builds, we feed off each other's excitement, both of us getting giddier and sillier. By the time lunch is over and we're walking to science, we're positively hyper—Cassie squeaking in a Minnie Mouse voice—neither of us caring who sees or overhears, just like in fifth grade.

It isn't until we get to class when I stop. "Oh no."

Cassie sees my face and halts, too. "What is it?"

"My backpack."

Her expression immediately becomes serious. "Let's go look."

We speed-walk back to the cafeteria, Cassie assuring me the whole way my bag's surely still under my chair right where I left it. I want to believe her, but I can't help thinking of the video Dad made me watch when I got my cell phone, about how important it is to keep your eyes on your things, because somebody could snatch them at any time.

But of course Cassie's right—my backpack's still in the cafeteria. Only, now it's shoved under a chair two tables away from where we sit. We trade worried glances.

"Just noticed it myself," Mr. Olansky, the lunchtime supervisor, says. "Was going to finish locking up, and then look for an ID."

I thank him and check inside, trying not to panic. In the small front pocket are my house keys, and my money purse—nothing missing from that, including my library card, which may not matter to anyone else, but matters a lot to me. My phone is still in the elastic-edged inner pocket too, and nobody would want my pen case, since it was a gift from Leelu and therefore is covered with pictures of Doc McStuffins. The main section of my backpack—the one with my tablet, my notebooks, my books and other binders—still gapes open. But everything's there too, except—

"What is it?" Cassie says, seeing my face.

My stomach detaches from my body. "My diary, Cassie. I think it's gone."

Chapter Three

Mr. Olansky lets Cassie and me search for my diary under all the cafeteria tables, and even offers to look through the trash for it. I want to cry, picturing the cover's beautiful marbled Italian paper stained with pizza sauce, or its pages soaked with half-drunk milkshake, but if it's in the trash at least I'd know my secrets were safe, instead of being pored over by whoever might have taken it.

"You have to get back to class," I tell Cassie, trying to be rational.

"And you should get a pass to keep looking."

I tell Mr. Olansky I'll be back, before Cassie and I walk in glum silence together to science. It's good Cassie knows not to try and make me feel better, because I'm not sure anything can make me feel better right now. My diary is like my best friend—more than my best friend, since I write things in there I would never even say to Cassie. It's where I've poured out absolutely everything, no matter how angry or ugly or embarrassing, including—my body prickles with horrified heat—all those details about Tyrick.

When we get back to science, I tell myself not to freak out, that I'll surely find it, and ask Ms. Tasker for a pass to go back to the cafeteria. Luckily, she is not only brilliant but also very, very nice, and she writes me one without hesitation. When I return to the lunchroom, Mr. Olansky has already gone through one of the three bulging trash cans with no luck, but he tells me he's had to do this many, many times, for lost retainers or phones, and hands me a pair of latex gloves.

Picking through people's half-eaten sandwiches, soggy hot lunches, and discarded pizza crusts is gross, but at least it gives me something to focus on, until we get through the last bag and my desperate hope of finding my diary is dashed and ruined.

"I'm sorry, kiddo." Mr. Olansky pulls off his gloves and tosses them into the last bag. "Most of the time, we find what we're looking for."

I thank him and throw away my own gloves, trying hard as I can to steel my face until I can be alone. So many horrible thoughts are swirling in my brain about who might have my diary now, or what they might do with it, I'm not sure I can breathe. Thank goodness there are bathrooms right outside the lunchroom doors. I slip inside, rush to the last stall in the row, lean against the wall, and cry.

I don't say anything to Cassie after science, because we both know neither of us can say anything that will make a difference. She lets me slip down the hall without more than a wave, and for my final periods I try to make my mind as blank as possible. At the last bell, though, Cassie's somehow gotten out of her own class early and is waiting outside the chorus room for me. I'm surprised, but also relieved, and when Aja and Evie pass us and wave goodbye, I can even manage a small, genuine smile.

"I thought I'd walk you to the pickup," Cassie says.

"But you'll miss your bus."

She shrugs. "You might need company. I'll call my dad."

"Then you'll have to wait for him, silly. We could give you a ride if Leelu didn't have dance."

Cassie winces in sympathy. Leelu's dance means I have to do my homework perched on a folding chair in the corner. "Are you sure you're okay?"

"Go ahead." I'm not exactly sure I will be okay, especially if I don't have my diary to write in about how awful today has been, but there isn't anything Cassie can do. "I should probably study for math. And I can always read."

"You've got *Little Women*? For comfort?"

I pat my backpack. "At least they didn't take that."

We're at the top of the hall, where she needs to head right and I need to head left, but Cassie hesitates again, giving me a sympathetic look.

"Really, it's okay."

She's still worried. "Call me later?"

I nod. She squeezes my hand, and clearly doesn't want to leave, but she really needs to catch her bus.

"Sissie, you take forever," Leelu groans when I hop into the back of our nanny Maritza's car with her.

"Shut up," I tell her, fierce.

"Maritza!" she hollers, startled just as much as I am by my own ugly tone.

"Both of you, quiet." Maritza's voice is tense. While she drives a giant Suburban, and has been in Monterey since she moved from her tiny Texas town six years ago, traffic still makes her nervous. "Fiona, you know about that kind of language."

Instead of answering either of them I take out my phone

and text Mom: **Something bad happened in school today.**

So sorry to hear that, she types immediately back. **I'm just getting out of a meeting, and have some things to wrap up before I meet Rachel for dinner. Do you want to talk on the phone before bed?**

I guess, I tell her.

You are a beautiful rose surrounded by carnations, she says, trying to make me feel better. But right now all I feel like is a bramble of twisted thorns and weeds.

Trying to study during Leelu's dance practice doesn't help. It's difficult to memorize anything with Leelu and her friends floating around the studio to Jason Mraz anyway, but especially with all the horrible questions swirling in my mind about my diary. Who has it? Why did they take that instead of something else, and what are they going to do with it? Do they even know who I am? Did they do this on purpose? And if so, why? Out of panic and fear I check the school message board and all my feeds about a hundred times, waiting to see if whoever did this might be bragging about having my diary, or even posting passages there, but nothing shows up. I text Cassie too, hoping that she'll quell my mounting fears, but her battery must be dead again because she never texts back.

At dinner (salads picked up on Dad's way home, but at least we're eating together at our own dining room table, and there's no Jennifer this time) Dad asks us how our days were.

Before I can say anything, Leelu says, "Fiona's in a bad mood."

"Is that right?"

Normally it's nice that my little sister knows my moods so well, and wants me to feel better, but there's no way I can talk to Dad about this right now, especially since I'm not really sure how bad it all is yet.

"Just school stuff," I say.

"Is anyone giving you any trouble?" he wants to know.

I shake my head. *Not yet anyway.* If I tell Dad what really happened, he'll just give me a disappointed lecture about keeping better track of my things. And then he'll probably insist on coming to school so we can report my missing diary to the principal and the school security officers. Dad could have them do a search of everyone in the entire school if he wanted to, and that would only make things worse than they already are. Nobody would ever forget a mandatory locker search for something like a diary. Probably I'd still get teased about it at my high school graduation.

"Well, if things don't improve after a good night's sleep and another try at it tomorrow, I hope you'll let us know."

I mumble something that could be interpreted as a yes, and excuse myself to my room. In my desk drawer are three more journals people have given me for my birthday or Christmas, since everyone in my family knows I like to write, but I don't want any of those diaries—I want *my* diary: its soft, blue-swirled-with-lavender cover and perfect-thickness paper. And I want my mom not to be out with a friend so she can make me feel better. Most especially, I want Cassie to call me back. I've tried three times since school got out, but she's still not answering, and I need her to help me troll the internet and make sure no one's broadcast my most private thoughts all over everywhere. But after looking at the same sites alone over and over, there isn't anything to do but try to study. Still, before I go over my notes, I flip to a random blank page in my plain notebook for English, date it, and write two single words:

Today sucks.

The first thing I hear when I step off the bus the next morning is a high-pitched voice squeaking, "Oh, Fiona, there you are!"

My diary anxiety made it hard to get to sleep last night, and when I finally did, I had strange, shadowy dreams of being lost in a giant concrete maze. Evie has to grab my arm before I realize it's her talking to me.

Her eyes search my face. "Are you okay? I heard what happened. I'm sure it isn't as bad as it sounds. Everyone knows Izzy always has to exaggerate everything."

The mention of Kendra's best friend and head minion makes everything jerk to attention. "Izzy?"

Evie's face shifts from worried and shocked, to embarrassed and uncertain. "You mean Cassie didn't tell you?"

"Didn't tell me what?"

Her mouth twists to the side. "Didn't tell you what happened yesterday, with your diary. It wasn't really Izzy, anyway. More like . . ."

She doesn't want to say it, and I don't need her to. The apologetic agony in her eyes as we move into the hall makes it plain: *more like Kendra Mack.*

Immediately I want to sink against the wall, and huddle in a moaning, humiliated heap. If Evie already knows about my diary this early in the morning, then it means pretty much everyone in the entire seventh grade could, possibly more. But if Kendra and Izzy really have my diary, the last thing I need is someone catching me bawling in some video on their phone.

"I heard it from Blake," Evie explains. "She told me Jordan was on the bus with them when it happened. Kendra had your diary and she and Gates were . . . they were messing around."

Her vagueness only makes me panic more. "What did they do?"

"Well, you know what a show-off Kendra is." Evie tries to downplay. "Always so dramatic."

"And?" I demand, picturing Kendra and Gates pitching my diary all over the bus, batting it to everyone on board. When she hesitates, I put my hand on her arm. It is thin and cool and the exact color of dried-out pine needles. "Evie, the homeroom bell's about to ring, and I need to know what I'm walking into."

She looks at the ceiling as though the words will be written there for her. "She was reading parts of it out loud."

Something takes over me, and I start walking down the hall, fast. Evie's calling out, but I'm already a span of lockers away from her.

"I'm fine." I wave behind me. I think I even smile. "I'll talk to you more in chorus, okay?"

My feet are walking one-two-one-two fast and hard, though I'm not sure where to yet. Because if Kendra has really read my diary out loud on the bus, there's absolutely nowhere I can hide.